ROOKIE IN LOVE

MAINE MAULER HOCKEY SERIES

ZOE BETH GELLER

KINKY INK PUBLISHING, LLC

Rookie in Love:
Maine Mauler Hockey Book 1

ALL THE FEELS ROMANCE

Please visit my website at zoegellerauthor.com

❀ Created with Vellum

FREE BOOK! TYLER: HOOKED

Tyler: Hooked

https://geni.us/FreeBookTyler

This is a short story to introduce you to the Sin Bin Hockey Series of 10 books! Get yours free today!

DEDICATED TO MIKA

We miss you.
2011-2021

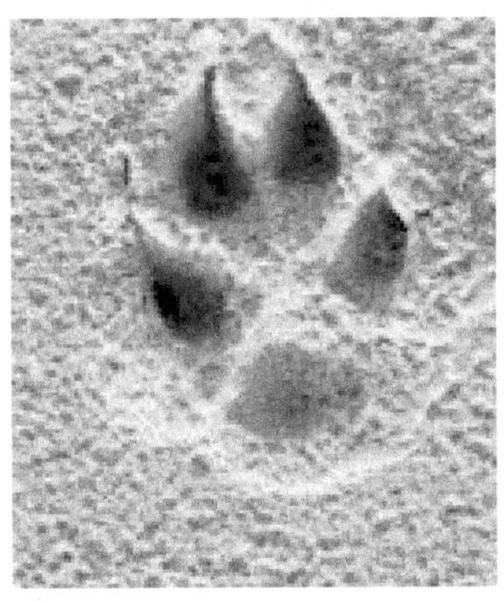

PLAYLIST FOR ROOKIE IN LOVE

Playlist for Rookie in Love

https://open.spotify.com/playlist/4Uszlg8bVAtA0HY9Ng4CEr

Havana (Feat. Young Thug)
Camisado (Panic at the Disco)
Beach House (Chain Smokers)
Danza Kuduro (Don Omar, Lucenzo
Mrs. Robinson -Remastered (The Lemonheads)
All Star (Smash Mouth)
South of the Border (feat. Ed Sheeran,Camila Cabello & Cardi B)

1

WYATT

"Hey, Rookie." I hear coming from someone on my right. I turn to see Alexandre, our right wing. "Hey." I'd love to respond using his nickname, but I have to admit I haven't learned it yet. This is all so new.

"That was a good game, eh." and I hear a bit of his Quebecois accent.

"Thanks, man," I return my attention to the bartender as he pushes a pint glass of Stout together with a shot glass full of equal parts whiskey and Irish cream towards me.

"Drink up," Alexandre instructs, joining me at the bar. We're the first to arrive at this dive of a place the guys think of as their second home. It's your standard sports pub: wooden tables, chairs, and a few booths. An American flag and signed hockey jerseys cover the walls. The large-screen TVs are the best in the area. People around here tend to be down-to-earth farmers and shipbuilders. Camden Hills isn't as affluent as a larger city, but watching sports while eating burgers and fries is as popular as anywhere else. Right now, the TV is tuned to the game, which affects our standing in the league.

For a sleepy town this low-key, I'm surprised to find the back room has, not only darts but axe throwing too. I guess you have to get rid of the stress somehow.

I stare at the Irish Car Bomb in front of me and, while it's very kind of Alexandre to buy me a drink and no way will I refuse it, I don't know why the guys come here if they aren't going to drink the craft beer which is advertised as being made on the premises. Fuck me. The thick as fuck beer and strong whiskey is a bad enough combination, but now they're trying to kill me by adding Baileys to the mix. All of this late at night after a stellar game.

Seriously, why couldn't they just stick with the house-made craft beer? I see three vats in a room, and it's blocked off to the public. They must be good because one is bottled and sold in the grocery stores alongside big-name brands.

I haven't been drinking long enough to like whiskey. I'm nineteen and not even of legal drinking age. Underage drinking is something we, as players, get away with, no questions asked. Call it a team courtesy. I don't ask questions, they don't ask for ID. Coming here as often as we do, I'm sure our bar tab covers more than half the owner's overhead.

"Fucking whiskey, man. You're old enough to drink this shit. I'm barely old enough to drink," I say, keeping my voice down to avoid the other patrons hearing I'm underage. That wouldn't be cool.

"Ha, well, get used to it," he jokes. I overhear a girl sitting on my left who mumbles she finds his accent sexy. If the look on her face indicates the level of heat in her panties, she's ready to slide off her barstool and follow him home.

Christ. Women hear any hint of an accent, and they're swooning.

I'll give him that: Alexandre is pretty good-looking, and an incredible athlete even at twenty-nine. When others his age might be starting to decline and finding it harder to maintain their position on the first line, he's still on top of his game.

Someone comes up and claps me on the back, "Good goal, rookie!"

"Thanks!" I shoot the Jameson Whiskey and Baileys to the back of my throat and chase it with the dark brown beer as the guys chant, and I guzzle.

What the hell? It's winter, and there's not much else to do here except eat, fuck, sleep and watch or play sports. And of course, drink.

Our goalie, Luc McDavid, did a hell of a good job on the ice tonight. We all tapped his pads to say thanks after our win against the Detroit Brawlers. It's only the third major league game I've played in, and tonight was extra special because I scored my first NHL goal. I'm still totally stoked about it.

McDavid is a fantastic goalie, and we're lucky to have him. He's over six feet tall, and his legs go from post to post. His goals-against average and save percentage stats are second to none. But if you've been around hockey players long enough, you know goalies can be a bit …strange. Fun, funny, weird, moody, they have it all going on. And you never want to piss one off. Well, I think that applies to all jocks, but especially goalies.

More guys arrive, and we move to a table large enough to accommodate the eight of us. We've earned a break after four wins in a row, and tonight we are in the mood to blow off some steam before two well-deserved days off.

In typical hockey fashion, we order everything on the menu. Copious amounts of food begin to show up at the table, from cheese balls stuffed with jalapeños to loaded tater tots, steaks, beer, and liquor. You name it, it's on the table. The banter flies, and the guys make me feel welcome in my new home. People keep congratulating me on my first NHL goal, and I'm on cloud nine.

The evening is just winding down when I notice a girl walk in. Even bundled up for winter weather, she is hot. Her long legs, blond hair, and full lips get my attention. Her jeans fit her like a second skin, and she's got a body with curves in all the right places. As she strolls towards the bar, all eyes in the room are checking her out. And when she bends over the bar to talk to the bartender, I decide she's a girl I'd like to know better.

Even though I've paid my tab and am about to follow my teammates outside, I decide to make a detour.

"Later, man." I give a nod to my teammate, and he acknowledges it by putting a hand up. When he opens the door to leave, I can see the snow has picked up again. Great.

I'm used to brutal winters in Michigan, but damn if Maine isn't showing me a new low with this subzero weather. February is just around the corner, and I'm told we're due for some more dumps of snow and even colder temperatures. Let's just say I could use someone to help me warm up in this weather.

I approach the pretty girl without a name. "Hey, how are ya?"

"Oh, hi." She smiles and turns towards me. I figure she's around my age.

"What's a young lady like you doing out so late?"

"Oh, well, everyone ditched me, and I feel like shit." She smacks her gum, and I feel she's already had a few drinks.

"Want a drink to talk about it?" I'm a gentleman and have time to spare.

I just moved here and live alone so I haven't really made friends yet. The team is a team, and getting to know each other takes time.

She thinks for a few seconds, then tosses her long blond hair onto the other side of her face in the classic 'I want to be picked up' move. Honestly, she's practically the one coming on to me.

"Great, let's grab a table."

She follows me to a booth, and I order her a beer since she says that's what she was drinking at the last place.

I order a beer too, but I don't need it. I'm still a bit buzzed so I take my time sipping it slowly.

"So, bad night, huh?"

"You could say that." Her lips are in a pout before she looks at me. "Say, aren't you the new kid on the team?" She snaps her fingers a few times, clearly trying to remember my name. I take pity on her and help her out, she's cute.

"Yes, yes I am," I say, extending my hand. "Wyatt, nice to meet you."

She takes my hand with a tiny giggle. "Sylvia, likewise."

She pulls a cell phone out of her oversized Coach bag and makes a face when the screen is blank. I find it odd when she flips it face down on the table, like, what is she hiding? But I shrug it off.

She's drinking, so she must be at least twenty-one. I don't like the idea of her driving buzzed, but at the same time, I'm not her keeper. For me, I don't want to be behind the wheel until I'm beyond positive I'm sober enough to drive. So I nurse my beer, allowing time for the buzz to wear off. Now that I finally made it into the NHL, I can't derail my career with a stupid DUI charge – or worse, an accident with injuries.

After spending so many years working towards a career in the NHL, it's surreal I'm actually here and making good money. I was schooled on the road and didn't have much time for a life outside of hockey while I traveled around Europe on the U.S. Juniors team, hoping I'd be spotted by a scout who would let me try out for the pros.

For now, this new life doesn't include a steady girlfriend. I've been too busy practicing on the ice with the team, hitting the gym, and all the other shit that has to get done. But once I'm settled into this new routine, maybe. The problem is that any girlfriend must be prepared to spend most of her time without me. I have a great life but a wonky schedule.

That said, I wouldn't say no to hooking up with this hot little number.

"Did you see the game tonight?" I take a stab at the fact she might like hockey.

"Oh, yeah, I go to most of them. I love hockey," she drags the word love out for emphasis. "By the way, Congrats on your first goal. You must be super happy."

"Thanks," I reply. She was paying attention to the game, I'll give her that.

We sit in awkward silence.

"You want to come to my place?"

"Sure." I get the feeling she was waiting for an invite.

I slide behind the steering wheel while she scoots into the passenger side of my utility vehicle, making sure her snow-covered boots are on the floor mat so as to not mess up the carpet. That's considerate.

I wanted a convertible sports car, but we're in Maine, and I was advised to get a practical car because you can't drive a sports car after the roads are salted.

I was disappointed, but I had to agree. We have the same problem in Michigan, so I got this used Tahoe for real-world use. In the meantime, the Mustang sits in the garage and only comes out to play during the warm months.

I turn on the radio for background music because I'm not sure we have anything to talk about. I put the car in gear and drive carefully as the roads are slippery. I need to get used to driving on snow and ice again, like when I lived in Michigan. Getting to the NHL is such a rarity for any player I can't jeopardize it by sliding into a ditch.

I pull up to my gated community which is home to numerous high rises. The security gate reads the barcode on my car and goes up automatically. I just bought a pretty expensive condo, hoping that I'll be successful and be able to stay. I'm cash-poor right now, but I can always sell it if I don't cut it.

Sylvia follows me into my place. It's devoid of furniture or anything personal because everything happened so fast. I closed on the unit, moved in a few boxes of shit, and have had no time to look at furniture.

"Nice digs," Sylvia says with a smile as she lays her animal print coat on the kitchen countertop and asks for water.

"Sure, I do have one set of glasses," I lightheartedly announce as I grab a clean glass from the cupboard over the sink. I fill it with ice and filtered water from the fridge door and hand it to her as she slides her phone into her purse.

"You just moved in, or….?"

"Um, yeah, sorry, I don't have much yet," I admit, wondering if she's ready to bail and call a cab or Uber.

"Do you have a bed?"

Now we're talking.

2

EMILY

It's freaking glorious that while the rest of the country is suffering through freezing winter weather, I'm basking in the warmth of South Beach. I inhale deeply as the waves crash ashore, listening to the rhythmic vibe that I know so well. This is what Sundays should be about, relaxing on the beach and decompressing.

I spread a beach towel on my ergonomic lounger and take a seat, kicking off my flip-flops. I love the warmth of the sand as I flex my feet and wiggle my toes. Heaven.

Rubbing my feet together, I knock off the excess sand before lying back. This lounger could be used as a bed, it's that comfortable. I look up to make sure I'm fully under my umbrella. I picked this umbrella with its pink and blue colors as it reminds me of the bright and colorful Art Deco buildings that originally made this beach famous. The colors were made popular again in the 1980s with the success of the TV show Miami Vice. Today, they're used on our local NBA team's jerseys. Some things just don't change, and I'm okay with that.

I pull up my long blond hair and plop an old Fedora on my head. My hair still looks good from being blown out for Friday night and I want to keep it that way. I don't like those big floppy hats that a lot of people wear. They make me feel old and if they get water on them, they lose their shape. The Fedora is a classic look and I think it goes with the vintage vibe.

Comfy and settled, I pick up my alma mater tumbler filled with boozy orange juice and take a few swigs. With my thirst quenched, I hold the tumbler in one hand and balance it on my long, tanned leg while I take in the view. People watching here is super entertaining, and I enjoy looking at people of all shapes and sizes strolling along the water's edge.

The sign says No Dogs, but I can see that lots of people are ignoring it. Just watch where you step, is all I'm saying.

Miami is more accepting and inclusive than most American cities, and it's not uncommon to see same-sex couples walking hand in hand along the water. I watch one couple leave their footprints in the wet sand until the next wave washes them away.

Latin music can be heard coming from one of the bars along the strip. In my peripheral, I notice some shirtless young men putting up a volleyball net near me. Hum, I slide my sunglasses down my nose and check out the new scenery. Yummy.

Pushing my Ray-bans back up my nose, I pretend I didn't just check them out. This is my place, these are my people, and this is my perfect Sunday.

There are plenty of tourists here; it's Florida for Christ's sake, but it's beginning to feel like 'tourist season' is a year-round event. As long as the snowstorms rage up north, the roads will be extra crowded, and so will the beach. That's why I usually get here early. Today I waited on my girlfriend, but I had to leave without her, or I'd never have gotten a parking spot.

The office building where I work isn't far from here so if I had to, I mean really had to, I could park in my spot there and hoof it, but with the chair and cooler on wheels, it would be a challenge for sure.

As a local, the water is too cold for my liking in February. I know every single person in there right now is probably visiting from somewhere cold: Germany, Canada, or Minnesota. There's no way a Floridian is going in the Atlantic until Memorial Day. That's usually a very hot weekend, and the Ocean will warm up a bit before then, but one can't count on it.

I lean back and look out over the beautiful blue ocean and observe a young couple frolicking in the surf. I smile, watching them having fun, splashing each other, and then hugging and kissing, entwined. I can't believe they're not freezing, but then again they've got each other to keep warm.

I detest cold weather. I'm born and raised right here, and even though my boss wanted me for his New York office, I talked him into letting me stay in Miami. I could care less that I don't have all the supposed glamour associated with an apartment in Manhattan.

What glamour? The thought of living in one room that serves as my kitchen, living room, and bedroom does not appeal to me. I don't need to lie in bed and cook eggs at the same time, y'know? There's no parking anywhere, and it's insanely expensive. Sure, there are lots of cool things to do in New York City, but there's cool stuff here, too. And with today's technology, I'm only a video call away from meetings if need be.

It's a bit ironic for someone who loathes the cold so much ended up working for a sports agency that represents all kinds of jocks in all kinds of weather, like football, basketball, and just recently hockey players. I'm one of a handful of attorneys on staff: I work mainly in public relations. I enjoy it more and I get to work unencumbered by office politics. Plus, I can watch the parade of the sports figures visiting our Miami offices without having to entertain them outside of my fundraisers. It's perfect.

I don't like entertaining clients because I loathe small talk. I'm not into superficial fluff and prefer to initiate conversations where I get to actually know a person.

If I'm spoken to, I have no issue speaking my mind. That sometimes backfires. I'm trying to be more diplomatic in the office, but it doesn't come naturally. My public relations finesse comes in handy when a player gets himself in hot water, and I help Dan out with solutions. What can I say? We tell it like it is most of the time, you know? No sugar coating for me, it takes too much effort. On the plus side, I work in a man's world, and they don't mince words, so I fit right in.

The one thing I'm not 100% down with is that on top of the job I was hired for, I was also assigned the girlie tasks around the office, like organizing office parties, ordering coffee supplies, and other stuff like that. It's sexist, but I can't get ahead if I'm not a team player. At least I get to order the coffee I like.

The silver lining, right?

I apply copious amounts of sunscreen to my body for an even tan without patches of burned skin and double check to make sure the umbrella is keeping the sun off my face. No need to age prematurely.

As I reach up to adjust the umbrella, a volleyball lands in front of me and sends sand into my face. I spit out some granules, trying to make it look as ladylike as possible because of all the hotties next to me. My face feels like it got a sandpaper facial and I glare at the GQ style jock, who mumbles a hello before trotting back to his friends. Are they models, athletes, or just good-looking hunks who happen to be next to me? I'm prepared to soak up the view however, being hot doesn't exempt them from having manners.

I'm a bit peeved at having sand all over me, but it's a public beach so I can't really get mad. But usually, these mishaps are followed by an apology and an invite to get a drink, so I'm even more annoyed because there wasn't even an apology. Am I losing my touch? Shit, I'm only twenty-eight, screw that! I still have time —don't I?

Between the sun glaring off the ocean's surface and the rising humidity, it's getting a bit toasty.

Definitely time for a refill. I open my small cooler and fill my tumbler with ice and orange juice, then add the bubbly. So what if I catch a buzz today? Assisting the attorneys in New York with all the press releases and interviews associated with acquiring a smaller agency pushed my stress levels over the edge this past month. I'm so glad it's done.

It's hard to get into the sports management industry, so I can't complain. At the end of the day, I have a pretty cushy job. I let the pros sign the players, and I only need to negotiate with them on small details in their contracts. Or they send me in with the bad news their agent doesn't want to tell them, like they aren't being re-signed, they need to retire, or, my favorite, 'we're looking at other options at this point.' Then I run with the agreed dialogue to the press.

If you're picturing a female version of the character Joe in *Ballers*, you've got it.

The sports stars can be high maintenance, but it's paying off my student loans. I handle our fundraising and charity events because I have easy access to so many players who participate. One hand washes the other, so to speak.

And my boss, Dan, is always booking a new project that I end up handling. Dan is super talented at signing new athletes to the agency. He's a retired NFL quarterback from the Seattle Saints who won the Super Bowl three years in a row back in the '90s. I met him in a bar on South Beach when he was visiting Florida, and in the two years I've known him, Dan has become a close friend and a second father figure in my life.

I glance over my shoulder and pull my sunglasses down again, trying to decide if the guy who looks familiar is the husband of some reality star. Nope, don't think so. As much as I'd like to entertain the thought of what a night with one of the hotties would be like, that's as far as it would go. I'm getting set in my single ways and wonder if I'll be able to give up my freedom to live with a significant other. I can't remember my last boyfriend.

What is going on with the volleyballers? Those dudes are chatting up girls younger than me. How did I become so unapproachable at such an early age? How did that happen so suddenly?

I'm sure by volleyball dude standards I'm a geek supreme compared to their steady diet of filet mignon – chicks that are perfect in every way with their fake boobs, fake nails, fake tans, and fake eyelashes. I'm not prepared to use Gorilla glue to affix body parts if they don't appreciate my natural curves, to hell with them.

I don't exactly have an hourglass figure. I'm more of a Chianti bottle — the one with the wicker bottom. I clean up well, and I have designer clothing, but it wears me, I don't wear it.

I turn my attention back to the turquoise ocean so I'm not caught staring. Taking another sip of my drink, I lean back on the small pillow attached to my lounger with Velcro and watch the wispy white clouds float by without a care in the world. Lucky for them, they have no deadlines and aren't micromanaged by older, more 'seasoned' clouds.

"There you are," a familiar voice says at last.

"Natalie!" I'm happy she showed up. She's my best friend, alter ego, and younger than me.

She looks like a goddess standing over me. You'd think she had a glam squad put her together, but no, she's just that beautiful. She's of Latino descent. I love her warm skin tone and the fact that she can speak two languages fluently. I'm not half bad, living in Miami you have to know some Spanish, and growing up here made it easier to learn.

"Girl, this is awesome," I enthuse as I take in her outfit. Her tan pops in a fuchsia bikini, and the sheer beach cover-up makes her look even sexier than if she had nothing on. She looks red carpet ready with her hair in a perfect chignon. No wonder she's late, who knows how long it took to pull herself together. But that's just Natalie. Forget fashionably late, she's always more than an hour late if she's a minute.

Somehow she manages to get to work on time. She's the secretary at the office and still attends night school at the junior college. What was I thinking to invite the younger competition to join me at the beach? Kidding. She's a doll, and I could use a pick-me-up since the guys seem oblivious to me.

She is definitely on their radar, so maybe I can be her wingwoman and wrangle a date out of this morning yet.

3

WYATT

I wake with a pounding headache, my least favorite thing in the world. It reminds me of when I was playing in high altitudes like Colorado. A frozen lake above the tree line always made for perfect pond hockey. The thin air gave me headaches and a dry mouth no amount of water could quench. If I had to choose, I'd rather suffer from the altitude while playing pond hockey than from drinking one too many Irish Car Bombs. Jesus.

I hear snoring and roll over to find last night's hook-up sprawled on her back with her mouth open and a fake eyelash stuck to her forehead. It all comes rushing back to me. I glance around the room, taking inventory, and see her shoes and clothing strewn across the floor from the door to the bed.

A cold chill rolls off the windows and infiltrates the room. I head to my closet and pull on sweatpants, a light thermal shirt, and a matching jacket that I zip more than halfway.

My pounding head reminds me that I need water and coffee, stat. Opening the bathroom medicine cabinet, I grab a few pills for my headache, cup my hand to catch some freezing water from the faucet, and toss my head back, swallowing everything at once.

I have a coffee machine that grinds the beans and makes any

type of coffee drink imaginable, so I go for the big guns and make an espresso. That ought to perk me up. As soon as I finish the cup, I hear a loud yawn.

Sleeping beauty must be waking up. I walk to the bedroom and lean against the doorframe, "Hello."

"Oh, Hi," she says as she props herself up in bed and runs her fingers through her hair in a failed attempt to make her bed head go away. "What time is it?"

"Eight."

"Oh, crap, it's Monday. I have a nine o'clock class!"

"You're in college?"

"Yeah, I go to Longfellow University."

"Cool."

I only took a few online courses to get a base of knowledge if things didn't work out with hockey. Now that the pros have picked me up, I have a choice to continue with school or just say fuck it. I'm inclined to go with just saying fuck it.

"Can I get you a coffee?"

"Not unless it's in a to-go cup, sorry," she says, springing from the bed. She scrambles to pick up her clothes and puts them on in the correct order. She's having a hard time with her sweater. Her first attempt ended with it on backward. I withheld a snicker as she accidentally knocked the eyelash off her forehead. I consider picking it up off the floor and returning it to her, then think better of it. Like, are those things even reusable?

She was pretty loaded last night. I'm wondering if she's okay to drive. DUIs in Maine are no joke.

"Are you okay? To drive, I mean?"

"Yeah." She pulls her hair from her shirt collar, sits on the bed, and pulls on her socks and boots.

"Coat?" I ask as she stands up.

She looks at me at long last. "Please." She smiles.

I walk to the other side of the bedroom, pick up her coat and purse, and hand both to her.

"Thanks." She reaches in and whips out her car keys without even looking. I'm amazed. Most girls can't find anything in their purse.

"Hey, can I ask —what was up last night?" I'm curious why she picked me and why she hasn't asked to see me again. Things are not adding up.

"Oh, that. Well, I was pissed last night, decided to have a few, and thought, screw it." She turns to look me in the face. "My boyfriend was ignoring me, I was pissed off at him, that's all." And she gives me a kiss on the cheek and turns to leave.

"Who's your boyfriend?"

She looks over her shoulder. "Cole Barber, defenseman for the Longfellow Whalers. I gotta go." And just like that she's out the door.

Wow, this is the first time I've been used for a one-and-done hook-up. Scratching my head, I don't know if I should be offended or impressed. Whatever. I go back to the kitchen for another espresso. The frost on that chick left me with a different kind of chill.

Then it hits me: Did she say her boyfriend is a hockey player?

Fuck!

What is Sylvia's agenda? Drawing the attention of a jealous boyfriend on the town's college team is not how I envisioned my first week here playing out. Pranks, yes, a lonely woman using me for a revenge fuck, definitely not.

Clearly, Sylvia knows the lay of the land. Why me? She must know who I am. Now I feel like an idiot. More importantly, I worry my budding friendships are in jeopardy after last night's stunt. The hockey community is tight, and everyone knows everyone, but they don't know me well enough to know I wouldn't do something like this intentionally.

Between the Sylvia stress and the second cup of coffee, my stomach is giving me fits, so I eat a protein bar to try and put out the fire.

Fuck! If I'm not already, it's only a matter of time before I'm on the shit list. I have a weight training session in two hours. That's two hours of pacing and waiting to see if this is going to blow up in my face. Plus, I imagine some of the guys will be there working out.

I figure there's no harm in getting to the gym early. I pack a workout bag, grab a water bottle, and head to the state-of-the-art facility. When I open the door and walk in, the chlorinated air from the indoor pool hits my nose, clearing my sinuses.

"Not a good day, man," Alexandre says from where he's doing squats, watching himself and me in the mirror.

"What?"

"Dude, just don't let McDavid see you. He's not going to be happy."

I approach Alexander and ask, "What's going on?"

"Rumor going around you fucked his sister last night, and of course, her boyfriend is on the warpath," he fills me in.

"Dude, seriously, I had no idea who she was," I claim ignorance, knowing they aren't going to care.

"Doesn't matter, you know that." He finishes a set of squats with 300 pounds on the bar. Holy shit, I have work to do if I want to catch up with the big boys in the weights department.

With a loud clang, he puts the bar back on the stand and walks me to the door. "Think you might want to lie low this morning."

"I have to meet my trainer. I can't leave," I explain, feeling my chest tighten, enraged that this little piece of tail used me to make some prick jealous, and now it's fucking up my entire life.

I've had it!

"Fuck that chick, man." I throw my hands up in disgust and defeat. "And fuck women in general. I'm not dating or getting involved with anyone. That's it! Damn, if I can't trust someone I had sex with, who can I trust?"

"To be honest, Wyatt, you only knew her for two minutes. And if you swear off women, you're going to get horny as fuck, and that will screw up your game."

"No way, I'm just going to be detached from all of it," I declare to Alexander, my only friend right now, as I release the air in my lungs and try not to punch something.

It seems to sum up my life right now perfectly.

All the wind is out of my sails, my entry into the NHL blemished, possibly ruined.

Fuck me. How did this happen?

The door swings open, and the team's trainer, Nathan Dumont, walks in. He's Canadian and worked with the Edmonton Enforcers before taking the gig here. Winters here can be just as cold as in Alberta. I'm not sure how much of an improvement this will be when it comes to winter weather. I hope he likes small-town living because Camden Hills is half the size of Edmonton.

Nathan is a tall and former hockey player, so he knows what we put our bodies through daily.

"Wyatt," he says with a smile and gives me his hand. It's not much of a smile.

"Let's head to my office. We can review the basics and see what you want from training and all that good stuff."

"Mr. Dumont." I shake his hand. "Sounds great."

"Call me Nathan," he says.

"Got it." I follow him out the door and down a hallway past a small medical room for guys who need quick stitches in the middle of a game and other stuff like that. Let's hope I don't find myself in there too often.

There's a network of locker rooms, the Zamboni path, and a medical suite. It's not colorful or fancy, but it gets the job done.

I can't get the Sylvia debacle out of my mind. Players need to develop a thick skin over the years because the guys who let things get to them on the ice are easy to pick on. Maybe I haven't developed mine as much as I thought.

I've got to devise a plan to get myself out of this clusterfuck. My life and my career depend on it.

4
____

EMILY

We had a great time on the beach, now I'm in the mood for a Cuban sandwich, so Natalie and I head over to a little joint we know that does an awesome job with their sandwiches. I love it pressed, with the bread thin and crispy on the outside, and that's just how they make them there.

"I'm surprised you didn't wrangle a date out of one of those volleyball players," I say, elbowing her while we're standing in line to order at Mama's Café.

It's a small spot in a strip plaza near the beach and even though the rent is probably ridiculous, there's nothing fancy about it. There are a few tables inside and a few more outside on the sidewalk. It might not look like much, and it's cash only, but it's well known for its home-cooked Cuban food. Her pulled pork is better than anything you get in a chain restaurant.

"Hi, Mamma," I greet the owner sitting behind the counter taking orders down on a piece of paper. All five of her kids work here, hence the nickname.

"Hola." She smiles. She understands more English than she lets on, and the majority of her clientele is Spanish-speaking.

We place our orders and wait for our number to be called while we sip from bottles of cold iced tea.

They used to make fresh tea by brewing hot tea and then letting it cool so it was natural. Once business picked up, they're too busy with the cooking and have to buy bottled drinks.

"I'm surprised you didn't pick up a mocha frappe on your way here," Natalie teases me.

"And spoil my appetite? No way," I exclaim. "I'm starving. Besides, this is enough food for the day."

"Who are you kidding? You know you're gonna have no problem demolishing that entire sandwich," she snickers.

She's right. Okay, I'm no waif, and I don't eat like a bird. Stress combined with sitting more and going to the gym less is gradually having a cumulative effect, but I'm fine for my age. I think.

"You're such a wench. We can't all be toothpicks like you," I goad her.

"As if. Besides, I'm younger. Wait until I get closer to thirty, then we'll see."

I sigh. "I can't believe the big 3-0 is so close. Damn, I have got to find a nice guy to date soon. You'd think with so many people in town, it wouldn't be that difficult."

"Even at school it's difficult. Good guys are like unicorns," Natalie agrees as our number is called. She picks up our sandwiches while I snag a table outside.

It's a perfect day. It's in the low 80s with a light breeze blowing in from the Atlantic. The overhead canopy gives me the shade I desire as I sit in my bikini with a cover-up that isn't too revealing.

There is a crazy variety of pedestrians walking by. Imagine South Beach being used to film an episode of *Bay Watch*, the movie *Cocoon*, and a hip-hop video simultaneously. That's Miami; we have everything going on. It's another city that never sleeps.

I unwrap my sandwich, peel back the waxed paper, and sink my teeth into the smoked pulled pork, slices of deli ham and pickles.

Mama's secret mustard recipe is the best part. A string of melted Swiss cheese stretches between the sandwich and my mouth. Fantastic.

"Oh, my," I moan. "This sandwich is always perfect."

"Okay, you're treating it like it's a sexual being. It's food, not a dude," Natalie states emphatically. "You need to get laid, girl."

"I know." I sigh, and my shoulders sink.

"You have to put yourself out there if you want any chance of a husband before you're thirty-five."

"Okay, now you're ruining my Cuban sandwich high." I pout as I stare at her and lick my fingers.

"I bet they use that Amish butter on the bread before it's pressed. Maybe that's Mama's secret." I try to change the subject.

"Okay, I see what you did there," Natalie smirks, winking at me as she takes another bite.

"Well, what do you want? A miracle? It's too early. Christmas just passed."

"Very funny," she mumbles with a mouth full of food. Her long brown hair falls perfectly around her heart-shaped face.

Her makeup is still perfect. How does she do that? If I wore makeup to the beach, it would slide off my face. Okay, maybe her makeup wouldn't be a match for a hurricane or torrential rainstorm. Apart from that, she manages to pull off the perfect look no matter what.

"Hey, I don't see you walking around with; what was his name? What happened there?" It just hit me that she's been showing up solo, and we never really talked about any breakup.

"Todd. I think we just wanted different things, and we're young. I'm in the mood to have fun. He's a bit older and wanted me to get serious about my finances and plan a 401K. He's a stockbroker, so naturally his life revolves around money talk."

"I hear ya," I say, rolling my eyes. She's privy to all the jock banter at the office. I don't have to elaborate. "Well, if it makes you feel any better, I have a ton of student loans and my salary doesn't go up as much as it does for the men in the office. That's something that I need to talk to Dan about."

"Damn, that's not right. He probably wants you in New York. Good luck avoiding that."

"There's plenty of qualified people in New York without me having to move. Besides, who else will do all the little extra things he bestows on me? If I'm not here, it will get dumped in your lap," I remind her.

"Ouch, rrrrrright." She lets that sink in and cannot argue.

I do a lot of the work that would otherwise fall to her, and she knows it, so I don't feel bad when I ask her to do my makeup before a huge publicity event, like the golf tournaments when all the stars and the staff from the New York branch blow into town.

"Honestly, Emily, you're great at what you do. You're a total catch. Maybe you should look at the guys that come through the office. I can find out who's single. You never know."

"I dunno. I'd hate to have a man that travels all the time. And the ones who are retired are going through one identity crisis after another. No, thank you."

"Well, your decision. They can't all be basket cases, is all I'm saying. There's got to be some good options out there." She lifts her tea to her lips and takes a few sips.

"True, never thought of it that way." I wad up the used wrapper around my sandwich and put it in the paper bag. I nurse the rest of my drink while Natalie finishes her sandwich.

"Maybe we both need to get on the dating bandwagon," I suggest.

"Um, well, yes and no. I have my eye on a few guys, we'll see. You, on the other hand, should join every dating app there is except the one that is strictly for hook-ups. Skip that one," she snickers.

"Oh, stop. Everyone gets hot and bothered from time to time. I mean, if you have an itch, it needs to be scratched, right?"

She all but spits her tea in my face and catches it by putting her hand to her mouth. I crack up at the comical sight.

"What? It's true!"

She swallows and wipes her mouth with the paper napkin.

"You just make me laugh at the most inconvenient times," she giggles, and the sound of her letting out a snort sends me into a similar fit.

I smile at her warmly. "I'm glad you're my BFF." I collect our trash and throw it into a garbage can on our way to the parking lot.

She's right. There are plenty of men out there. I just need to find one viable candidate, someone with a personality and someone who isn't into estate planning.

We give each other a hug goodbye and head off to our separate cars. I drive a BMW because in this business I have to look successful. It's a charcoal gray color, my compromise between black, that's too hot to touch with the sun, and white, which is too boring.

I open the sunroof in preparation for the bumper-to-bumper drive back to my one-bedroom condo fifteen miles inland, where I could afford to buy a place. The sun is beating down on me, and with traffic at a standstill I soon give up, close the sunroof, and turn on the air conditioning.

My phone dings with the ring tone from Ballers, and I know it's Dan. I sigh inwardly. His calls are rarely good news.

"What's up?"

"Hey, Emily, how's it going?"

"Good beach day. How about you?"

"Good, good. I see you put in the requisitions for the Weston Classic Golf Tournament."

"Yeah, it's coming up at the end of the month. Is there a problem?"

All major fundraisers and most golf events take place in February since that's the season down here. That's when the big money people show up and lots of the celebrities are in town for the beach. They double dip, mixing business with pleasure. Recruiting people to golf for these events is like selling frozen popsicles to a kid during a heat wave.

"No problems at all. I'll get these through and have my secretary book my flight down."

"Good, it will be great to see you," I say, already calculating what I should wear when the big boss comes to visit. The weather in February can go either way. It could be very hot or freezing. It's one of those months when we're likely to get a blast of arctic air from a polar vortex up north. Of course, 'freezing' in Miami is highly relative.

"Great, everything going well? The golf event all set?"

"Yup," and I inch forward a foot in traffic and eye an opening in the sea of cars ahead of me. I'm anxious to get home, shower, and chill with a good book or watch a movie.

"Okay, take care," he says before hanging up.

It's not like he doesn't check in occasionally, but it's rarely one way like it was today. Weird. Maybe he's just happy now that he acquired the smaller agency and is looking forward to adding more money to his bottom line, I dunno.

No sooner do I find a spot in the parking garage of my high-rise condominium than my mom texts. She lives in north Florida, where the state actually gets a winter, and apparently, it's cold there today, in the fifties.

Again, I know, highly relative, that's not cold for people who live in places like Minnesota. I learned all about blizzards and ice storms from the baseball players our agency represents. They used to have a spring training camp in southwest Florida. Whenever a player would talk about the weather back home, I would give thanks yet again that I don't live anywhere near there.

I hit the clicker on my way to the elevator, locking the Beamer. When I'm inside my condo, I immediately step out onto the balcony and take in the view. I insisted on it when I searched for a condo. I swear it's my favorite place in the house. Such a huge change from growing up in the sticks outside of Tallahassee, a stone's throw away from the Florida/Georgia line.

I'm proud of how far I've come. But I wouldn't mind getting a raise.

5

———

WYATT

I leave Nathan's office happy after our first meeting and head to the gym, checking first to make sure it's empty. After I work out for my normal hour, I head out and run into Alexandre, fresh from the pool and smelling of chlorine.

"Hey, man, any word?" I speak softly lest the walls have ears.

"No, but McDavid is pissed," he replies. His voice is on DEFCON 1, and I'm starting to worry.

"Damn, all I want is for this to go away. I've never had any problems anywhere I played."

"I know. But word about last night has gotten around. The goalie wins and loses games for us. We can't have him off his game over this, or it's only a matter of time before it goes up the chain."

"Fuck me," I grumble as we walk to the parking lot. "I seriously had no idea."

I'm pissed, and I hope I never see Sylvia again. It's like she ripped a freaking page right out of the movie *Major League*. I'm annoyed by her pathetic attempt to get noticed by a guy who probably isn't into her anymore. I'm a guy, and I know these things. That's how we operate.

"I gotta run," he yells as he jets off to his sports car.

"Later." I feel as cold and bitter as the wind hitting my face and wonder how people can act this way. I slide behind the wheel of the Tahoe and drive home, lost in thought.

I pull into the condo parking lot, and before I can get to the elevator, I see McDavid spot me on the way to his car. My day just turned into a nightmare. Sometimes it's nice that so many of my teammates live in the same complex; other times, I don't. This is one of those other times.

"I need a word, Hildebrand." His brisk walk means business. He does not look happy. Fuck, fuck, fuck.

"Look, I had no idea. I had no clue she was your sister or anything. I mean, I'm new around here. I'm really sorry." I put my arms up and shrug, trying to convince him of my innocence.

"Yeah, well, stay away from her, or I'll make your life miserable here," and he pokes me in the chest as he blows past me on his way to his car. Message delivered. I pray to the stars above that he lives in a different building in the complex. I don't exactly want to be sharing an elevator with him all the time.

I make a beeline for the elevator and check my surroundings for anyone else lurking in the shadows. Safely inside my condo, I make lunch and sit on a cardboard box in the living room to stream a show and decompress. Man, I gotta buy some real furniture.

There's bound to be more fallout from this incident. It's bad enough that Sylvia is our goalie's sister, but at least she's not dating one of my teammates. For that, I'm grateful.

I wonder if I should call my agent and give him a heads-up before he hears it from someone else. Maybe not. I'm still holding out that this doesn't go any further. And I don't really know my agent, which makes it tricky. A larger firm just acquired my agency. I have no clue who's representing me these days. I chew my nails uneasily.

It's starting to snow again, and a big part of me wants to hibernate like a bear until this Sylvia situation passes over. Then I think that might make me look guilty when really I'm not. Argh, no one wants to hear that. McDavid doesn't want to hear his sister is a bit out there and that she came on to me. Now that I think about it, no brother wants to hear that about his sister, even if it's true.

My phone dings. It's Mom—shit, not a good time. I'm not in the mood. I text her that I'm busy with training.

She's cool.

And so my day of dodging people continues.

At least Alexandre is making an effort to keep me in the loop, which is nice of him. I am glad I made one friend before Sylvia, the human wrecking ball, showed up.

By late afternoon I decide to pick up a pizza, but as soon as I leave the underground parking I can't miss the sports car riding my ass. If it weren't for my bumper, our cars would be kissing each other metal on metal.

What an ass! I wish he'd go around me but no, he's practically in my back seat. What a prick! The level of the car's lights are low, and I realize it's a sports car. This means he's really desperate to show off to have it on the road this time of year. It's also ironic because all hockey players drive sports cars. This is running through my head when I pull into the uneven parking that looks like the surface of the moon.

I park in front of the pizza joint and pound out a drum solo on my steering wheel. Listening to loud rock music never fails to lift my mood when I'm in a funk. When the song ended, I turned off the ignition and noticed a car pull up behind me, the same car that was following me.

I step out of my car, thinking *Here we go.*

"Hey, I want a word with you," he growls as he unfolds himself from the car worth over a million. This has to be Sylvia's boyfriend, and he's huge. He has to be a defenseman. They are usually the team's largest guys, except for a goalie. Goalies are just taller than hell.

"Look, she pretty much picked me up," I try to explain and quickly realize I said the wrong thing as he's here to defend her and stake his claim. I find it all ridiculously juvenile, and I wonder how fucked up their relationship can be and still be called a relationship.

"You're trouble, man." He moves towards me as he rounds the front end of his souped-up car and proceeds to get into my face to intimidate me, but I stand my ground.

"Never, ever, look her way again," he threatens.

I want to enlighten him about his girlfriend and how she played us. It's only a matter of time before she does it again, and she's probably done it before, but think better of it.

"No problem. I don't want any beefs with anyone," I assure him. If it weren't for my young career on the line, I would let him throw the first punch.

"Well, see that you stay away from campus," he spits before backing up.

"No problem." I hope it's a promise I can keep, but what if I want to take classes at the university? "I'd only be there if I'm enrolled. I want to reserve the right to pursue my education, if that's okay with you." It's the only quick thing I can come up with to throw it back in his face without escalating the situation.

"Yeah, we'll see about that. With the people my father knows, you'll be packing your bags before the week is out."

I stifle a groan.

So this Cole person is a bully. I bet he's a dirty player too. They typically go hand in hand. Eventually, they get kicked out of the league and banned from hockey. If that's the case, I hope he's kicked to the curb before he hurts someone. He seems to have some serious anger management issues.

I snag my pizza as Cole stuffs his body into his expensive car next to his buddy.

I throw the to-go guy a generous tip and return to my car. I wish the guys on the team would reach out, but that's wishful thinking for now.

I was told our team captain likes to promote camaraderie, and yet I'm not getting invites to do things. I even check my phone to make sure it's working. Oh my God, how pathetic is that?

I eat in front of the TV and try not to worry about being traded next week or being sent to the minors as punishment.

～

THE STADIUM DOESN'T HIT me between the eyes and have the same 'wow' effect it did the last time I entered it for a game. I have a bitter taste in my mouth from the drama and politics swirling around. I just want this to be over.

The locker room is too quiet. I gag on the stench of smelly skates and unwashed hip pads on the dude next to me. Someone is popping bubble gum, and it's getting on my nerves. It will take me some time to figure out who's who and what their various pre-game quirks are, but it's not going to happen today.

Tension hangs in the air like a thick fog. I steer clear of McDavid. It's a shame because I like him. I hope to God he's got his head in the game. I'm praying for him to have a perfect game, and for the first time since I arrived, I care more about his game than mine.

The guys throw some one-liners at each other, and a water bottle flies across the room. I piece together from snippets of conversation that many of the guys went out for beers and axe-throwing last night, and I'm disappointed I wasn't invited. But it doesn't really come as a surprise.

It's also not a surprise that I'm at the back of the line to hit the ice as we line up in the tunnel. I just keep my head low like anyone would do in my situation: duck and cover. It's not the first time this has happened, and it won't be the last. Some other poor schmuck will get it on the next go around somewhere in the hockey universe. It just sucks that on this go around, I'm the poor schmuck.

I do my routine stretches once I hit the bench area and catch McDavid in my peripheral vision stretching his groin muscles and hammy's before taking the net. He seems focused. We're playing the Toronto Twisters tonight. They're having a good season: they are in the running for the President's Cup and will most likely go all the way to the Stanley Cup finals.

Meanwhile, we're clinging to the bottom rung of the Wild Card position. We still can make it to being a team in the top four in the Atlantic Division— if we get enough wins. Every game counts.

Tonight, I need to put everything else out of my mind and focus on scoring and helping the defense out as much as possible so our goalie wins. I mean, we all win, but he needs to have a stellar game more than anyone because my actions might have fucked with his head, and that's not good.

McDavid is loose in the net during warmup. I don't know him well enough to read him properly. The fanfare at the beginning of the game starts like always, and I get into the pop music of Smashmouth and enter what I call The Wyatt Zone. That's the headspace where it's only me, the ice, the puck…and the bodies I have to skate around and outmaneuver.

I cut past a teammate who's not trying hard enough to get out of my way, and I have to do a quick deke around him. So that's how it's going to be. Okay, fine. I turn it up a notch and have an awesome game, adding another goal to my stats.

Like they always say, 'take it out on the scoreboard,' and I did. I might be young, but I'm not stupid.

Despite my best efforts, we lost 5-2. McDavid didn't have a good night, but we still tap his arm or goalie pads before we skate off the ice. The guys are in a funk returning to the locker room, and I think it best to remain quiet as I head to the showers.

I'm in my world under the water when I get hit by an open beer can that makes its way over the shower wall intentionally or as a prank. It's like an unsuspecting missile attack, and I'd like to think it's the guy's way of including me.

Okay, fuck it. I pick it up and open it, spraying it inside the shower before guzzling it.

Shower beer, why not? I'm sweating, and my face is red, but the hot water feels good. The near-frozen beer feels even better. Honestly, I'm surprised more hockey players don't end up in rehab.

The guys are loosening up with banter and verbal zingers, but it gets quieter again when I enter the room to get dressed after my shower. A beer can flies, and McDavid's name is called. The can lands on the floor, and beer spray goes everywhere, so Luc has to guzzle a can of beer. That's the way it works. If the can had landed straight up with no beer spilled, the person who threw the can would have had to guzzle it.

"Fuck, you guys are the worst," Luc complains as he pops a top and downs his beer.

I'm not part of the shenanigans, and I make my way to the door without so much as a word. Outside the locker room, one of the assistants says the Coach wants to see me for a minute.

Oh God, this can't be good. I dutifully follow him down the corridor until we reach an office full of signed memorabilia from Hockey Hall of Famers on the wall. Coach is sitting behind a huge desk, his face stoic as usual.

"Hi, Wyatt." He stands, motioning for me to have a seat.

I unbutton my suit jacket, sit on the edge of the chair, and feel like one of the three bears in Goldilocks. I'm tall, the chair is small, and I have muscular thighs from all the weights and skating I've been doing since I was three. I look about as uncomfortable as I feel.

"What's up, Coach?"

"I heard a rumor, and much as I'd like to stop it from going to the top, I can't. The family involved are friends of the GM, and they donate a ton of oil money to his favorite charities."

"Yes, sir." Inside I'm like, *Fuck me, I'm so screwed.*

"I want you to stay, but Luc didn't have his head in the game tonight, and I think we all know why. Usually, I like to give these things time to blow over, but we can't afford any more losses. I called your agent so you can be represented, and maybe he can smooth this over a bit."

"Thank you, sir."

"Yeah." He leans back in his oversized leather chair and rubs a hand over his clean-shaven face, "These things happen. I don't like to interfere with the team, but a loss is still a loss, and we're on the cusp of making the playoffs."

"Yes, sir, I understand."

"Okay, your agent will be in touch, probably fly someone in, but don't worry, it's to salvage the situation, not to facilitate a trade," and he stands to shake my hand.

I stand, giving him a firm handshake and wondering at the same time if he's telling the truth or if I'm on the next bus to a shit team – or worse, down to the minors.

"Have a good night, and keep up the excellent training. Dumont tells me you're doing great."

I pause before exiting the room, turning half my body towards him, "Yeah, it seems I have tons of free time these days, so I try to put it to good use."

He nods, and I take my leave.

It's freezing outside, and I regret not bringing a jacket. It's a short walk to my car, and I look at my phone out of habit. Nothing.

6

EMILY

After a refreshing shower, I settle into my overstuffed sofa, turn on the TV for background noise, and call my mom. One thing about living alone is you really notice how quiet it is. This building is only full during peak tourist season because it's a second or third home for many retirees. The rest of the time, it feels like a mausoleum. Seriously, the entrance to the lobby is all white marble and would look like a huge bidet if not for the oriental rugs and potted palm trees. I'm happy in my modest condo for now, but there is no way I'm meeting my future husband here. Just sayin'.

"Mom, how are you?"

"Good, you?"

"Fine, fine, except my knees hurt when I garden. I'm getting older, and I swear the ground is getting harder. There was not much rain this week, but we got a cold front."

I'm not surprised. She's over six hours north of me, and there can be a huge difference in temperatures during the winter.

"What do you have growing in the garden?" Like, I don't know, but it gives her something to brag about.

"Oh, my Heirloom Beefsteak tomatoes are too perfect to eat!

They are huge and take their time to turn red. The only thing is, I don't know what's getting into them, squirrels or bugs, but something is eating them like they are candy." I hear the exasperation in her voice.

"You got me there, Mom, no idea. That's way outside of my wheelhouse," I say. I can't even keep a damn orchid alive, and supposedly I don't even have to water it, but once a month, it should have been easy. After I killed my sixth plant, I gave up. I've accepted the fact that I didn't inherit my mother's green thumb.

"I know, but you know me." I can tell she's upset about the unknown villain snacking on her tomatoes.

"Yes, I do."

She's a perfectionist, just like me. I totally got that from her. It's a personality trait that helps me in my field through contracts for events and insurance company riders. I'm surprised I'm not wearing glasses yet, given all the fine print I read looking for mistakes and loopholes. Come to think of it, sometimes I'm the one who crafts the loopholes.

I take a sip from my water bottle, which reminds me I should hit the gym on the second floor. It's not very fancy, but it has the basics to work out and tone this aging body. A stationary bike, treadmill, and some free weights are more than enough to keep me busy for an hour. It's getting to the gym that's the real challenge.

"Were you at the beach today?"

"Oh, of course. There were some clouds and a light breeze, making it bearable. This is my favorite time of year. The rest of the year, it's always so hot." I'm telling her what she already knows, but she understands I love where I live and wouldn't want it any other way. "I didn't have to sweat to death to enjoy the beach," I chuckle.

"You are a toe in the sand, salt in the hair kind of girl. How's work?"

"Fine, stressful, we're growing and adding smaller companies."

"Well, that's good for your job security."

"Yes, it is," I agree, and she's right. "Oh, and the good news is that MLB isn't having a strike this year so we don't have to contend with the added stress of our player's futures while we worry about our own." Strikes and lockouts are bad for sports in general.

There is a brief pause. "Any promising dates lately?" Ugh. I knew that was coming.

"No, it's hard, Mom. You'd think there would be plenty of single men in this city, but it's getting harder and harder to meet men."

"You mean cute men."

"I mean men that are appealing and single," I correct her.

"Right, well, I'm ready for grandchildren, you know. Maybe then I could get your father to leave the house, and we could take a road trip to see you."

I let out a considerable chortle. "As if that will ever happen."

"I know, he hates long drives," she admits. Mom has resigned herself to the fact that Dad is a homebody. Plus, like most men, he hates change.

"He really hates to leave the house now that he's retired, doesn't he?"

"Yeah, and he needs a hobby. All he's been doing is puttering around the house. He's so in love with the new grand-baby and has plenty of time for more." It's not exactly a subtle hint of the wish for more grandkids. Does she think I will start popping out kids because Dad needs something to do?

"Mom," I drag it out to emphasize she's nagging again. "It's depressing enough to be single in my soon-to-be thirties, never mind that I'm the only girl in the family who doesn't have kids yet."

It's not that I don't want a family eventually, but for now, I'm content. I plan to pay off my student debt and maybe branch out on my own so I have more flexible hours. It's not like I don't have a social life. I have Natalie and some college and law school girl-friends to hang out with.

The one thing I'm lacking is a vacation. I could use a break. The trips to the beach are keeping me sane, but I need to get away and kick it up a notch. I should dust off my passport from my trip with the girls to the Bahamas last winter, or…shit…was it two winters ago? Damn.

Mom updates me on my older sister Jane and my brother Billy. Billy is playing football on a scholarship at college in Gainesville, and Jane is still happily married to her high school sweetheart. Mom loves that Jane still lives in town, and I like that one of us is super close to our parents as they age.

Shortly after hanging up with my mother, I fell into a coma induced by the sun and the belly full of that delicious Cuban sandwich. My power nap is longer than expected because it's dark outside when I glance outside my sliding glass doors.

I needed the sleep. I've been working many late nights at the office, helping to crunch numbers with the lead team as I am their second set of eyes when they have major deals. Add to that the finalization of the golf tournament contracts confirming details with vendors and rental equipment. I've been a bit stressed.

A few weeks ago, I was working late to review the buyout of Athletes, Inc. to ensure we didn't miss any details. The name sounds like something right out of an ACME cartoon. I can't believe they were a solid company filled with mostly hockey players.

The name might need help, but their bottom line is very good, and that's what attracted Dan. The company has some big-name hockey players as clients, and I heard about a new hyper-skilled kid they just picked up, too. They say he can 'shoot in any upfront position' and is 'a strong two-way player,' whatever that means. I'll be reading more hockey contracts to help me navigate public relations events and press releases. I had hoped that I'd pick up the jargon by osmosis. Heck, maybe I'll even go to a game. Dan can get me free tickets anywhere.

When it comes to football and basketball, the meat and potatoes of our company, I know pretty much everything. Because all the star athletes love Miami, I get to meet quite a few of them and their wives when they visit.

As for golf, that's different. Dan loves golf. That's his jam, and he likes to oversee those contracts in New York, which is fine by me. I could care less who hit what and the number under par. For me, the most action on a golf course is driving the carts or checking out the cute caddies. But there's a lot of money in it, and it's extremely popular in Florida. The snowbirds play in winter, and the locals like to book the links early in the morning in the spring and summer, just after the sunrise, because it's cooler that time of day – and the green fees are more affordable.

The large annual golf tournament is taking place the last week of February, and Dan as always is looking forward to coming down for it. He pays for a tent and a private lounge for the players that's off-limits to everyone else. He likes to rub elbows with all the golfers looking for agents and possibly steal some away from other agencies if they're not happy.

For me, it's an annual event that I run for the company, and it's a rinse and repeat type of setup. I know all the key players that come every year, but I try to get new athletes from our agency to partici-pate to change it up. Then publicize the hell out of it. I arrange for nice giveaways, raffles, items to auction, you name it. It's all for charity. It gets us free media coverage and keeps our company name out there.

I should get moving and pull myself upright, but I'm still exhausted. What is wrong with me? I can't keep my eyes open, and I say screw it. I pull the soft throw over my legs and drift back to sleep.

I'm having a lovely dream when my phone rings, and it's Dan's ringtone. I knew it. His call earlier was just to butter me up before he puts me on shit detail.

I fumble in the dim light cast from the TV playing a rerun of *Dallas* and finally find my phone. "Hello?"

"Oh, thank God I got you, Emily," he says. He's in full-blown panic. I've never heard him so stressed out before.

"What's wrong?"

"I got a call to meet with that new rookie we just picked up in Maine. He's involved in some kind of mess over a girl, and I guess it's upsetting the team's dynamics. I was going to handle it, man to man, but I just got in a car accident, and I'm heading into surgery for my leg. I need you to fly up there to take care of it and do what you can to smooth things over. You're the best at public relations. He's a good kid. He's new to the NHL. He might need some extra hand-holding."

"I'll go right away. But Jesus, Dan, I'm sorry you're hurt."

Fuck. I have a trip lined up, but it's not a vacation. Oh no, that would be too much to ask for. I'll be going north in February, the dead of winter, to Maine, of all places. The closest I want to be to snow is sitting in front of a roaring fire inside a ski lodge. And I would not be there to ski. I would be there for the apres-ski.

"I'll be fine. I have to go." I hear sirens in the background. Poor guy, he must have been in one. He gives me the name of the airport I'm flying to, the kid's name, and a few small pointers before he hangs up.

Just when I thought my job was returning to a normal workload after the acquisition, I was thrown this curveball.

Why me? Then I remember that most of the guys at the office have families, and the rest are too new to handle this. With Dan out of commission, I guess he'll need his experienced staff in New York to run the office.

And that leaves me. Tag, you're it.

Shit.

I call my office manager and leave a message on her machine

that I'll be out of town and using my company credit card to entertain clients and pay for emergencies.

I'm wide awake now and hope Dan will be okay. I doubt he'll make it to the golf tournament seeing as how he needs surgery. But I have his back, and I pump myself up to do this. Problem is, I have no fucking clue what I'm actually supposed to do. Agents usually handle the hand-holding and advice-giving, but I don't act as an agent, and I'm not used to young jocks. I assume the kid needs some good publicity, but I'm not convinced that he's such a good kid. I'll have to take Dan's word on that.

Do I see the men finesse the players at lunches? Sure. Do they kiss their asses at times? Check. Do we put out fires? All the time. I need to be prepared to turn all that snow up there into water to put the flames out for this rookie.

I'm in uncharted water and have no idea what to expect except for a very long line at the airport tomorrow and a mess of cold and snow at the other end. The flight I just booked on my laptop is jam-packed, and I'm not happy about having to take the center seat. I'll see what I can do to change that to a window or aisle when I get to the airport.

Next, I pull out my suitcase and wipe off the dust. It has a loose wheel, but it should make one more flight. I didn't replace it because I haven't been using it. I'll put a new suitcase on my birthday wish list.

I will need lots of warm clothing. I rarely wear the stuff I keep it under my bed in one of those space-saver bags. Sitting on the floor, I pull out the bag and go through my sweaters. I have a down vest in the hall closet, and I'll need to see if I can still get into my tights. Ugh, tights.

I don't have much winter clothing. My only option is to layer what I have, wear my leggings and knee-high boots, and hope for the best. I just don't want to wear something that screams ill-prepared-tourist-from-the-south.

With everything packed and lying in bed, I'm finding it difficult to fall asleep just three hours before I have to get up. I keep looking at the alarm clock and can't decide if it's jitters or I napped too much. One thing I know for sure, there's no way I'm going to the airport without picking up a mocha Frappuccino with whipped cream along the way.

7

———

WYATT

I haven't heard from my agent, and the number I have continues to go to voice mail. I don't know what to do with myself. I have every video gaming system known to man and yet I'm bored and feeling left out, because I'm usually hanging with the guys or playing hockey.

Even when I go to the gym, all I get is a stellar view of my teammate's backs, and hear crickets when I walk in the door. I feel about as welcome as a turd in a swimming pool.

It's clear that Sylvia's games have branded me a troublemaker, and I'm being ostracized. I'm being punished without having a chance to plead my innocence. The hockey community is similar to a small town. It's not how much you know or how good you are at what you do, it's the powers that be and what they want and who said what to whom. Granted the stars of the teams get more leeway than a rookie in these matters, but it still comes down to management decisions.

I'm not calling my dad as he's so proud of me, and I don't want to worry him. Plus, I have a brother at home who's still playing locally, and I don't want him to be distracted by my drama. I got this.

Fuck it. I didn't get this far by being afraid to color outside the lines. I can man up when the situation warrants it. Right now, I need to be in control of my life and keep myself occupied. What better way to do that than go out on my own to explore?

There has to be some pond hockey around here, and it's not that difficult to load up my old equipment because the team's equipment manager had all my new gear – sticks, swag, you name it– hanging in the locker room, my first day here. It was great to arrive and find all that taken care of, but at the same time, I'm branded as a member of the Maine Maulers. I have to represent them wherever I go and do whatever they tell me to do for publicity. That will take some getting used to.

The NHL is not as strict as the military, but sometimes I feel like my life isn't my own anymore. I know success rarely comes without a price, but I seem to be paying the price before I've even had time to enjoy my success.

I'm not sure what I'll find once I get out of the burbs and into the more isolated areas. With it being so cold, only hardcore hockey players will venture out.

I pack a cooler with drinks so they don't freeze in my car. That's how cold it is, and I don't want them to explode. I layer on clothing as I walk around my bedroom, and as I pass the bathroom, I grab a jar of Vaseline and throw it in the cooler. No sense in letting my face get chapped from the wind.

I toss the cooler and my well-used hockey bag into the back of the Tahoe and drive to the skating rink near our arena. I ask around and get some intel on where a frozen pond might be. Typing the address into my car's navigation system, I hope that I get lucky.

Sweet! A chance to play pond hockey like a normal guy and not the new rookie on the pro team.

I'm excited to get out of town, but the snow is starting to come down thick. I debate going back home in case this turns into a blizzard. The thermostat in the car says it's already negative two outside, and it's predicted to drop lower tonight.

My phone rings. I answer it on Bluetooth.

"Where are you, man?"

"Out in the wild."

"Well, stay safe, and don't let your giblets freeze off," Alexandre laughs.

"I've got a line on a pond hockey game."

"Sweet, the one that's about thirty minutes outside of town? I think it's called Crady Lake."

"That's the one, I have it on GPS."

"Okay, well, be careful of black ice on the road and fucking elephant size moose, eh? You hit that, it's worse than getting hit by a train. I'm serious."

"I know."

Fucking moose, again. Like, our team logo is a moose for heaven sake. I'm on thin ice with the management. What else could possibly go wrong?

"All right, well, let me know when you get back, maybe we can grab a few beers."

"Thanks, I appreciate it, man."

"I wish I could do more. It will work out, you'll see. Sylvia isn't very reputable. It'll blow over."

"I hope so." His words of encouragement make me happy. It's good to think that I have at least one person on my side. I'll take that as a win.

"I'll let ya go. Later."

"Later."

The snow flurries are getting worse by the time I find kids standing off the side of the road and a bunch of cars parked close together. This must be the lake, and I follow the car tracks in the snow and park. I can see the pond in the distance and wonder if it gets cleaned off by a machine. With the way the snow is coming down, it would take too much energy and effort to shovel by hand.

Kids are congregating around burn bins scattered around the lake. There are also a few low-to-the-ground portable fire pits. Other than that, it's pretty bare-bones. There are no warming huts like I've seen in Michigan, nor any benches to sit on and dress while being sheltered from the freezing wind.

Instead of benches, they use plastic lawn chairs with rubber bottoms on the legs to prevent sliding. Metal chairs are to be avoided unless you're looking for a good sled. During the warmer months, these chairs are probably used for soccer and football games.

I put on my skates and dress by the back of my car, trying to stay out of the wind. No one knows me here, so I throw on my old hockey jersey.

I plan to just stroll out to play like I'm any other nineteen-year-old, not a professional athlete. Maybe that's what I need, to act my age and just cut loose. No one has to know my deets.

I trudge through the snow until I make it to the first group of young men who I assume live nearby. There are no tents or concession stands selling stuff, so this must be just a local pick-up game and not an official tournament. Perfect.

"Okay, if I join?"

"Sure, I'm Mac," says a lanky teenager around my age. He greets me with a fist bump.

I'm feeling better already.

"Hi, Wyatt."

He has chew in his mouth and spits in his water bottle. Most guys just spit on the snow, but that grosses out the girls so some use plastic bottles. Lots of guys chew, picking up the habit in middle school or after they get their first taste on a road trip. Me, I don't really care for it.

Mac and I drag the small box we're going to use as the 'net' to one end of the ice while two other guys set up a second one at the other end.

The ice can get slushy if it's a sunny day and it gets too warm, but I don't see that happening today. This shit is rock-hard.

Hell, even Camden Bay itself is frozen solid. With it being frozen over all winter, there is no way to harvest the lobster, so they'll grow undisturbed. Then by late summer or early fall, they'll be full-grown and meaty. That's when people all around the world flock in for a week of parties and music for the annual Lobster Festival. I'm told it's a blast. I hope I'm still here for it.

This ice is frozen but uneven, kind of like a frozen chop across the lake, and the snow is falling so fast the lake is covered, and I can't really glide.

Introductions are made, but I probably won't remember anyone but Mac. We pick teams, my jersey is close in color to one of the teams, so I join them to keep it simple.

We head out to start There is no contact so it's not much of a face-off. Pond hockey is played more like a game of sauce.

When I get the puck, I lift it in the air and chip it into the box. I'm all ready to celebrate, but I don't see that black puck anywhere. When I look down, I find it's still sitting in the snow under my stick. *Shit.*

And this is how it goes because the snow is covering the ice faster than the guys can shovel it. I hear the wind whip up and the chatter of the guys sitting on their chairs catching their breath. It's hard to breathe with the cold air burning my lungs. We're young, but it's kicking our ass so much that I'm counting this as a conditioning exercise.

Suddenly, I quickly flick one in the 'net.'

"Yay," I smile and raise my stick in a quick celly.

"Good one, rookie," says Mac. I told him I never played before, and that's the truth when it comes to pond hockey. Well, maybe once, years ago. Then life got busy, and I never got a chance to do it again. Now, I'm getting a feel for it, and we're getting to know each other a little and start throwing around some one-liners and zingers. It's fun, low pressure.

It takes all our energy just to battle the elements, but I feel invigorated.

Mac is smart and drinking something hot to warm himself up. There are no portable toilets, and guys are baptizing the trees instead. This is totally a guy's game as it's rough moving on the pond, not that girls can't do it, but I doubt they want to risk losing a tooth. This is hockey as wild, and it's as rough as it gets, and setting aside the fact that outside of Helsinki, this is the coldest I've ever been, I'm loving it.

I head back into the game. "Fuck! Mac, it must be like negative twenty out here, my nuts have gone turtle. They're so far up inside me, I can taste them."

"Get used to it, it's fucking Maine, this is how it is in February, we have snow five to six months out of the year. Where ya' from?"

"Michigan."

"Cool," he says as he passes the puck to someone else, and we score again.

We have a mini-celly, and damned if the other team doesn't turn around and score on us immediately. They're good at this.

I take a break so I can piss, but just as I am making my way to a tree, I notice a woman with long blond hair get out of a car and slam the door closed like she's pissed.

Crap, I decide then and there that I can hold it for a few minutes. This looks like someone is in trouble, and things are about to get interesting.

Mac walks up beside me. "You expecting anyone, Wyatt?"

"Hell no, I'm new here."

"Yeah," he says before he spits in his water bottle. "Women don't usually come out here unless it's an emergency or someone's dead." He chuckles, and the other guys on our team start throwing around wisecracks.

Meanwhile, Ms. Prima Donna navigates the ice and snow in her knee-high fashion boots. Between the boots and the leopard print jacket, she looks better suited for an MTV video than the backwoods of Maine. She looks high-maintenance, hot-tempered, and too hot to consider dating.

"She's gonna freeze that cute ass off" is just one of the many cracks I hear from the guys who have all stopped what they are doing to watch the new arrival. I want to chime in, but I'm captivated by how she's managing herself and can't take my eyes off her.

I can't see what her behind looks like, but judging from the frontal, she's got quite a package under that coat.

"I'm looking for Wyatt, Wyatt Hildebrand," she says like she's FBI serving a search warrant. She's not dressed like the FBI. What the fuck?

I'm stuck. These guys have to know who I am now, so my cover is blown unless I don't answer her.

Meanwhile, blondie is not winning her battle with the snow and tries to walk faster to get through it.

Wrong move. She teeters but recovers well. I'll give her an eight, It's pretty impressive how she pulls in her arms, just like a hockey pro would if he was losing his balance on the ice.

Then she yells my name again.

Jesus. Why can't I just have one afternoon without getting harassed? Are these Maine chicks so into pro players that they stalk the newbie?

8

EMILY

Luckily, most of the people at the airport are arriving as I stand in line to be felt up by security. These boots are great. The zippers up the inside make them easy to get on and off. It crosses my mind that it's been a long time since any man unzipped anything on me –or felt me up, for that matter.

The flight was delayed for hours due to bad weather, no surprise, so I'm relieved I don't have a change in time zones either. Hours late, I finally arrive at the small Portland airport. I'm startled to see a huge moose as I walk through the concourse. It's stuffed, of course, but still a bit unnerving.

Ugh, it looks dreary as hell outside, and there is no skyline. Typically there is a lineup of cabs outside any airport, but not here. Whether it's because this town is just that small or due to the snow, I don't know, but it's coming down pretty thick. I check my phone, and it says it's zero outside. That's not encouraging. I'd hoped it would be in the forties so I could make do with the few winter clothes I brought. Judging from the black cloud on my weather app and the white raindrops. I'm afraid I'm in for an extremely cold visit.

Great.

I'm flattered that Dan trusts me to handle this situation, and if I pull this off, it will give me bargaining power next time I negotiate a raise, but damn, why couldn't this be happening in Las Vegas or somewhere tropical?

I still don't really know what I'm supposed to do exactly. The only real advice Dan gave me was to give the rookie a break. Whatever that means. Shit.

I tug my luggage off the carousel. It was a small airplane so there were only about thirty bags on it. I guess not enough people fly here to justify a big airplane. Small airports and small planes make for short wait times, that's a plus.

My tummy growls. No food service on the flight sucks, but the food was never that great to begin with. I look around for something to eat, and that's a no-go.

Darn.

I'm hungry and thirsty from the dry, heated air. Indoor heat is something I rarely experience.

I pull a bottle of water out of my bag. I always travel with a refillable bottle because it's easier with airport regulations. I like to think that I'm usually prepared for most life events that go sideways. The humidity in the building is zilch, so I guzzle half the water.

I walk from baggage claim to the car rental counter to pick up my economy car. This should be fun. I requested a larger version of my car, a BMW Sedan. It's German-made and should have heated seats and do well in this weather. But they only have a limited selection of vehicles here. I get stuck with a sedan that seats five, so much for the perks.

When I open the door to exit the terminal, the arctic air steals my breath, and I have to cough to breathe or restart my heart. I'm not sure which. What have I got myself into?

Screw that. I got this!

I pull my coat zipper to the very top and wrap my scarf tighter. I don't understand how people can enjoy this frigid weather for half the year. I might as well be in Siberia. How long do I have to be here again?

I press the alarm button on the key fob to see which car flashes its headlights and find the one luxury car in the lot of twelve. I figure out how to open the trunk, chuck my roller luggage inside, and slide behind the wheel, shivering.

Now, to figure out the basics, lights, wipers. Do you use wipers in heavy snowfall? Fuck.

I feel like a rookie myself. I realize this car is newer than mine when I have to start it by pushing a button instead of using a key.

Of course, my Beemer isn't new. Who can afford that with student loans? It's a well-maintained older car that looks good for work.

Okay, I heard about this, what do I have to do to make it go? Push start, right? I chuckle at myself as it reminds me of South Park episodes that I watched as a kid.

Pushing the button does nothing. I pick up my phone and YouTube how to start this car. Oh, I need to put my foot on the brake.

Bingo!

The speakers blast rap music, and I scramble to turn down the volume and find a pop station. Then I turn up the heat to full blast to warm up and defrost my fingers and toes.

I look up the arena on my map and notice it's not that far of a drive. The team is supposed to have a practice today, so I'll swing by and see what's up. I hope all this can be resolved quickly. The sooner I can...do whatever I'm supposed to do to fix this...the sooner I can get my sorry frozen ass out of here.

After meeting him at a golf tournament a few years ago, Dan knows the general manager, but I doubt the GM will remember. Being a GM or owner means you meet a ton of people. Some you put in your phone, and others you discard like a one-night stand.

I pull out of the parking lot and follow the directions of my phone's trusty GPS as she narrates my trip and tells me what to do.

I could link my phone to the car's Bluetooth, but I can't be bothered and choose to forgo that hassle for now. With any luck, I'll be flying out tomorrow anyway.

Getting to the arena is easy enough, and I make a point of taking in the scenery along the way. I have to admit what I see is majestic, as the snow is fresh and not marred by exhaust. I cover the distance using country roads that are technically local highways, but by Miami standards, this is amateur hour. I'm starting to warm up and relax when the GPS announces *You have arrived at the destination.*

I park at the arena and go to a side entrance where I have to be approved by the person who buzzes me in after staring into the camera and having a short exchange through a two-way speaker.

Walking inside, I pass an office with two women who look like they might be secretaries or ticket salespeople. They barely look at me, preoccupied as they are debating the merits of homemade pizza dough vs. store-bought. I don't have time for this and hit up the security guard for some directions. He looks like a lifeline.

"Well, they pretty much left for the day, Miss," the older security guard behind the plexiglass tells me. "You might find a few that haven't gone home yet," he says, pointing towards the locker rooms.

"Thanks." I force a smile of gratitude. Not that he hasn't been helpful, but my day is getting longer by the minute, and I will get seriously hangry if I don't eat soon.

This is turning into some search and rescue mission as I'm resolved to find Wyatt myself.

I head towards the locker room, and the closer I hear a few voices and hope that one of them is a player who might know Wyatt. My luck has been shitty so far today, so I hope I strike gold as I knock on the door and crack it just enough to shout out.

"Hey, I'm looking for Wyatt, Wyatt Hildebrand. Anyone know him?"

The door swings open, surprising me as I stare up into the face of a player I don't know. Why would I, he's never been to our office, and we probably don't rep him. It's not like I'm the guru on all sports, there are only a few players I find sexy to watch. Most of the time, they are married, and it's a bummer.

"Hi." I smile.

Whoa. I can't refuse a man who smells good and is wearing a thousand-dollar custom suit. I mean, even Dan, on his best day, pales in comparison.

"Hi, Wyatt's on the healthy scratch list, so he wasn't here today," the light-blond stranger informs me.

"Oh." I step back and slide my purse back up my arm as it's intent on sliding down my winter coat, and it's beginning to irritate me. But what's more alarming is that things have clearly progressed from when I spoke to Dan. A healthy scratch isn't good for a rookie.

Crap.

"Do you know where I might find him?"

"Just so happens that I do," he smiles. "But who are you?"

"His PR person, I mean, I'm filling in for his agent, who was in a car accident yesterday. I'm just filling in," I scramble to explain.

"Hmm," he sizes me up with his deep-set eyes and square jawline, "I expected as much. He's a good kid. I'm Alexandre." He extends a large hand toward me.

I take his hand and give him a firm handshake as I imagine myself being Dan and wondering what he would do.

"Emily, nice to meet you."

His hand falls away, "He's at a pond where the locals play ice hockey. I texted him a while ago, he might still be there."

"Where is 'there'?"

"Place called Crady Lake."

"Is it on GPS?"

He chuckles. "Yeah, it's not hard to find. You can see it from the road."

"Thank you," I say and turn to go.

"Good luck, Emily."

"Thank you."

Damn hot players with sexy French accents. He's probably married. I say goodbye and head back to my car.

I should eat, but if I do, I might miss Wyatt. Then I would have to wait for him to call me back and probably not see him until around dinner time, giving me little time to talk to any of the higher-ups who make decisions.

I hit the destination Crady Lake on my phone and hit the road again. This rookie is hard to track down.

I turn my windshield wipers and hope my headlights are on. I don't travel much so I'm lost in these new cars.

I've never driven in snow before, and I'm a little freaked out. I mean, in New York, I always use subways and cabs. What does a Florida girl know about ice and blinding snow?

Fuck, fuck, fuck. I didn't anticipate being this far from the city and my five-star hotel. I wish I was in a truck as the road conditions are deplorable. The terrain is rugged with many rocks, creeks, and bridges, and the road bends around every single one.

But I am resolved to find him as time's a-wastin', and I really want to make my morning flight home tomorrow. Between the heavy snowfall and the temperature reading below zero, I'm not sure the flights will even operate.

I'm straining to see the road in the blizzard-like conditions when my phone tells me, *You have arrived at the destination.* I'm relieved because I'm not sure if I could have gone another ten minutes.

I follow tire tracks in the snow that lead to what I'm assuming is the pond and park alongside a line of cars that must belong to the slew of guys huddling around fires in trash cans. Seeing so many guys in one place looks promising.

I'm relieved to have found the place without getting lost or breaking down in the middle of nowhere.

The dial on my hangry meter is pegged into the red. There's a single serving of canned tuna with crackers in my luggage, but I can't bring myself to eat frozen tuna.

I don't know how anyone can enjoy doing anything in this bitter cold. In my opinion, grown men chasing a puck with a stick is more suited for children ten years old, max.

But hey, I'm getting paid because of all these man-children chasing inflatable balls and rubbery pucks. I would count my blessings if this weren't my first time doing damage control.

I kick the heavy car door open with my booted foot and get out. I immediately sink into the snow up to my knees. I don't know if the boots will ever recover. The wind assaults my face, and I pull the attached hood over my head as I slog the one hundred yards to the pond's edge.

There's no response the first two times I call his name, so for a third and hopefully final time, I call, "Wyatt, where are you?"

I catch some guys staring at me and realize I must look completely ridiculous wearing these boots in two feet of snow.

"Hey, who are you?" One of the young men asks, stepping forward. I wonder if this is him.

"Are you Wyatt?" I ask, trying not to sound confrontational. No sense in scaring him off. It's not his fault my flight was delayed, I'm under a lot of pressure, the weather sucks, and I haven't eaten.

The fact that his phone continually goes to voicemail, is probably the only thing I could blame on him.

"That would be me," he replies sheepishly.

"I knew it!" a tall kid beside him exclaims and slaps him.

"Sorry, man," Wyatt mumbles, and I wonder why he's apologizing.

"Don't sweat it, great playing with you."

"So, we need to go," I interject.

"Who says I want to? Everyone is pissed over nothing, and it's not even my fault. Just go back to New York. Besides, I thought Dan was my rep."

"Dan was in a car accident, and his staff in New York needs to run his office there. I'm from the Florida office and the person he wanted on this."

"Well, you don't look like you're cut out for it if you ask me." He quickly sizes me up, but something flickers in his eyes. A flicker of interest or contempt?

I square my shoulders against him as much as against the cold wind whipping over the frozen pond. It's like a page out of *Mystery, Alaska.*

"I'm not happy to be here either, Wyatt, trust me. And just put those eyeballs back in your head. I'm not here for anything but business. I'll be gone in no time if we do this right."

"What do I have to do?" He shifts his weight to one leg and looks down at my face, causing me to forget the cold for a moment.

Flames from the burn bin between us spit embers into the air, and they drift past us on the wind. I have a feeling that even if the fire wasn't there, there would still be sparks between us strong enough to ignite a burn bin of its own. Something about this Wyatt has lit a forgotten ember in my heart.

His brown eyes remind me of chocolate fondue, and I can't tear my eyes from them. Instead of thinking of work, his presence is provoking me to run right out and buy strawberries to cover us while I cuddle against his body for warmth and…I stop myself.

This kid is too young for me. Besides, I'm acting as his public relations agent right now, and I can't compromise the integrity of his case or fan the flames by adding to his list of sexual conquests, a list that is currently up for discussion with the GM.

What am I thinking? Why now? Why him? What's changed? Why am I suddenly feeling warm when it's below zero?

"We need to talk and make a strategy to fix it," I tell him even though I'm not exactly sure how we're doing that.

It makes sense that a new kid in town who is on the outs with his team would want to be with peers who accept him. And judging from the old jersey he's wearing and the other kid's obvious surprise to hear his name, they had no idea who he is. It's obvious he was trying to blend in and do what he loves.

We've all had moments like that. There's safety in being around people, even strangers, who understand us without asking questions. He's acting like an outcast wolf that's found a new pack.

My phone beeps with an alert from Natalie that the press has gotten wind that the rookie might be a healthy scratch for the next game and is sniffing around to find out the details as to why.

My day just went into the toilet. And I'm still hungry.

"How are you going to fix it?" he asks while packing up his hockey bag. Some guys are milling around on the pond, and others come by to shake his hand or clap his back for a good game or in appreciation of what he's accomplished. Now that I blew his cover, they know who he is.

"We'll figure it out. Because you weren't at practice today, the press got wind of it and are now hounding us for details."

He swings around and I see a mix of pain and panic in his eyes. "I don't want to go to another team."

"We don't want you to go to another team either," I assure him, but he's past being consoled.

He picks up his bag, gives some of the guy's fist bumps, gives the tall guy his phone number, and leads the way to the cars, "Well, I guess we're stuck in this mess together. I'd prefer Dan because I know him a bit, but one stranger isn't much different than another. Are you good at legal things?"

"The best."

"Then, I guess we'd better be going. Where to?"

"I'm starving, and I need food badly, anything to eat around here that we don't have to kill first?" I quickly look around to make sure there's no moose ready to charge me.

His chuckle is a combination of a snicker and a chortle, but it doesn't matter, it lightens my mood, and I find myself relaxing for the first time since I left the beach.

"We can find something," he says, opening the door to a large Tahoe that looks more like a beater car belonging to a college student than to a professional athlete. The door creeks loudly as he opens it and I notice the dashboard is cracked and the tint on his window is peeling. Maybe he's not one of those flashy players.

As he walks to the back of his vehicle and opens the lift gate, I can't deny I enjoy watching his cute ass. I plan to follow him back into town, so I need to hang out until he's ready.

I watch as he methodically unties his skates and chucks them inside the trunk along with his stick and bag. I wrap my arms around myself in an attempt to fend off the mind-numbing cold. My extremities have lost feeling, and my crotch is literally the only warm place on me. I'm sure my proximity to Wyatt is responsible for the fire below.

Wyatt stands abruptly and shuts the trunk. The noise brings me back to reality and to the fact that he's just a few feet away, and he's young, too young. But as he turns, our eyes meet, and my breath catches in my throat, and it's not from the cold this time.

"Follow me." He gives me a wry smile and climbs behind the wheel of his utility vehicle.

Whoa, so that's what it's like to have sexual tension. I'd never experienced it before. I never could understand why some women stay with their husbands going back and forth between breaking up and making up. Here I thought they were just being dramatic.

Now, I understand that maybe a part of them can't help themselves, that they're driven by sexual chemistry or a need so strong they can't break away. I know he's my client, and I shouldn't be entertaining these thoughts, but I cannot control what pops up in my head or the ache I feel in my loins.

His truck's exhaust is already going full blast when I can finally tear my eyes away and walk towards my nearby car. He idles his motor and waits for me to start my car like a gentleman.

Imagine that.

9

WYATT

I wasn't expecting a woman to show up instead of Dan. I'm not used to women calling the shots. I wish Dan had been able to come instead. We developed a friendship over the past few weeks, and he gave me good advice when setting myself up here. My parents are great, but they don't understand everything that goes into moving, having lived in the same house their entire married life.

I crank the heater in my car up to high while I sit, waiting for Emily to reach her luxury rental car. She's walking away from me, and for a woman who's been on the road all day, she still looks pretty damn amazing. She might be older, but it's hard to tell. The glowing tan on her face is a stark contrast with the snow.

I check out Emily's curves in her tight pants – or would I call those leggings? I can't tell from this far away. She's so ladylike in the way she sits and tries to knock the snow off her fashion boots before getting into her BMW. Priceless. She is entertaining, I'll give her that.

She's dressed a bit bougie for this neck of the woods. I bet she was going for a corporate look but didn't anticipate walking through ice and snow to find me in the middle of nowhere. She looks completely out of her element.

If the press is sniffing around now, I have no choice but to accept her help. With Dan out of commission, I have to take who I can get. I wish I didn't need her to get me out of the pickle jar I find myself in. The lid is on pretty fucking tight. In fact, I'm screwed.

All guys know that girls that look that good are high-maintenance. Big trouble, if y'know what I mean. I'm better off with someone more my speed, dependable, and down to earth.

Why am I even thinking this way? She's a professional sent here to fix my public relations nightmare. I shouldn't be entertaining any of these X-rated thoughts going through my head. She says she's good at public relations, and that's what I need right now. She's here to help clean up my damaged reputation, not make it worse, for Chrissakes!

I circle back to where Emily is warming up her car and ask, "How desperate do you think this chick is to piss off her boyfriend? I mean, do you think she'll make a public statement?" I'm worried she has an ulterior motive.

"She's probably done all she intends to. Knowing how girls think, she probably just wanted the attention and used you to make her boyfriend jealous. Classic move, and it seems to have worked, but we'll have to wait and see."

"Okay, well, follow me, and we'll try to find some food on the way." I'm trying to think of someplace that's convenient and come up empty because I've never been out this way. I ask my Bluetooth device to get a list of locations as I check my rearview mirror to make sure she's following me.

My brain is still turning over the whole Sylvia situation. My largest concern is for the family connected to the General Manager. You never want to piss them off. Players can get away with bad hits, suspensions, and tawdry behavior to a point. If you're one of the top players, you can get away with more and still remain golden. But this, I don't know. I have no idea if Cole Barber and his dad are going to try to sideline my career before I've had a chance to prove myself.

My internet symbol on my phone spins. I can't make a connection. It's supposed to be perfect, but things slow down in bad weather. Finally, my Bluetooth speaks to me with some places for grab-and-go fare as well as some places just off the interstate to get local cuisine.

We're about twenty minutes into the drive back when I notice I'm alone on the road. As in alone, alone.

She was right behind me. Where could she have gone? I turn the car around, concerned that something has happened. Fully anticipating finding her car in a ditch, I'm beyond relieved and a little surprised to see she has pulled off to the side of the road. She's standing in a vacated lot of snow-covered acreage, and for the life of me, I don't know why.

What now? I pull up behind her and put my car in park.

As I get out, I can see she's holding something moving. I hope to God it's not an injured animal. But as I get closer, I see it's a frisky, happy puppy. She's literally knee-deep in a snow drift holding a small German Shepherd pup. The dog has a tan and black face and looks like a purebred.

"How did you spot that? I was right in front of you!"

"I have no idea. I was looking at the pretty landscape and noticed something moving in the snow. I think someone just dumped it. Who could do that to a cute little guy like this?"

She pulls the dog into her heavy jacket to warm it.

"Let's stop at a store and see if we can get some water and maybe a can of dog food." Her greenish-blue eyes implore me and scan my face. She has dropped her big city façade. Now, she's just a kindhearted woman rescuing an abandoned puppy in a snowstorm.

She doesn't even need to ask because I love dogs, and she looks so sweet and loving with the puppy. Damn, makes me wish she was cuddling me.

"Sure, up the road is a gas station. I'm pretty sure they will have the basics."

"Great," she replies as I open her door for her. She carefully gets in, holding the puppy to her chest. She fiddles with the key fob before dropping it in the cup holder between the seats. After she fastens her seatbelt, I head to my truck and slowly drive the snow-covered road towards the gas station.

We park, and it's obvious Emily is quickly getting attached to the puppy because she's fussing over it like a mother hen. I open the door for her to enter the store, and she announces, "It's a female," as she walks past.

"Do I smell hot dogs? They smell good, and I'm hungry. Any left?" she asks, spotting the hot food section next to the register.

She's the last person in the world I'd expect to eat in a place like this, and judging from the cracked and dirty linoleum, I'm having second thoughts about eating anything in here myself.

I make my way to the rotisserie and find two taquitos that look like they've been there for days, and the one lonely hot dog is so shriveled it looks more like a breakfast sausage. Surely this stuff cannot be edible.

Emily peeks over my shoulder to check out the situation, and it's lumpy as I lift the lid on the hot cheese.

"Gross. I wouldn't eat that even if I were a contestant on *Fear Factor.*" I shake my head and replace the cover. I'm glad I looked first.

"I'm starving, but yeah, not that starving. I think we should pass. How about stuff for the puppy, though?" she asks as she walks over to an aisle. "Do you think someone will come back for her?"

Emily protectively pulls the pup up under her chin and giggles when it licks her face.

"I doubt it. It's sad, but someone figured she'd be picked up.

Maybe she's part of a large litter," I reply. "Sometimes people just suck."

"Seriously. If we hadn't passed by when we did, she might not have lived long enough to get rescued."

I see pet food and lead the way. All they have is canned food, so I grab a couple, a few bottles of water, and some paper plates on my way to the counter.

"Do you want anything?" I turn around to see if she's found anything to eat, and she's murmuring in the pup's ear. Oh boy. This dog ain't going to any pound.

I give the cashier my card, and we go outside to the sidewalk in front of the store. Opening the can, I put a small amount of food down and pour some water on the other plate.

Emily gives a questioning look at the tiny amount of food I've put on the plate. "We have to give her small amounts to make sure she won't get sick," I explain.

The dog looks about eight weeks old, meaning she has already been weaned. She takes a few seconds to lick at the plate with water before she moves to the other plate and inhales the food. Poor little thing was hungry.

I can tell Emily is starting to relax now that we have dog food and asks, "She's eating, that's good, right?"

"Sure is, but she'll need to see a vet just the same."

"Yeah, I know, thanks for helping," and she gives me a sweet smile that shows off her perfect teeth and kissable lips.

I'm not sure why it's important, but I'm glad she likes animals. Maybe I misjudged her. Other than our initial encounter, there's been no frosty shoulder, no complaints that the day isn't going as planned, no snarky comments about rural life, the sort of thing a man expects from a professional woman from the big city.

Girls tend to spend a lot of time on their hair, but she's not complaining about her gorgeous hair getting damp from the snow, drying, and then getting windblown. I find myself wondering who she is and what she's like, even as I tell myself for the thousandth time not to let my brain wander into this part of the forest.

"I figured you for a cat person," I blurt out of the blue.

She looks at me in surprise. "Oh, no, I grew up in the country, and we always had a dog. I kind of miss having one, but I have crazy hours and live in a high-rise. It's no place for a dog over five pounds."

"Well, we can get her settled at my place and call some shelters. I can order food for us and have it delivered if that's okay with you."

"Sure, I get cranky when I'm this hungry, but I'll make it," she assures me. "Until then, I'm not responsible for any smart remarks. It's been a long day, and you've been warned."

"I'm sure it would take more than you can dish out to scare me off. I'm used to being on a team of athletes that all have their issues," I laugh.

"Good," she says, and her relief makes me feel like I accomplished something today. One of the hardest things about not being a part of the team right now is that I feel useless.

"Let's get you to some food and this little one to her new home," I reply, running my hand over the pup's fuzzy head. When my hand grazes Emily's, I feel tingles run up my arm. We make eye contact, and I quickly look away. "I'll…uhh…just toss this garbage."

Emily takes the puppy for a quick walk in the snow to potty, and by the time we are ready to leave, the wind is whipping up again.

I check my rearview mirror to make sure Emily is following me and call a Chinese restaurant to order food. When we get to my guard gate, I instruct her to drive in behind me. She parks in a guest spot and waits for me to get her.

Ironically, she's rescuing a dog when she's supposed to be on a mission to rescue me. But I'd do the same thing. I have a fondness for all animals; this one is pretty freaking adorable.

I carry the pup while Emily has the dog food and water. As we enter my building, the concierge at the front desk greets me by name.

"This is beautiful," she murmurs appreciatively, looking around the huge lobby. There are separate corridors that lead to the various amenities, which are accessible around the clock.

"Thanks, I just moved in, so don't expect a lot of furniture at my place. Dan helped me get organized. He's a nice guy."

"He is. Thanks for your help with the dog. We don't have to drop her off at a shelter today, do we? It's getting late and all."

I sense her reluctance at parting with the dog, and I don't blame her.

"So, you rescue a dog, and now it's my mission, too. Is that how this works?" I tease her, momentarily letting go of the chip on my shoulder from the team's cold treatment.

"It would be great," she purrs, giving me a cute little smile that turns me inside out.

I can't say no.

That's a first for me.

We're just getting settled at my place when the concierge calls to say I have a food delivery, and a minute later, there is a knock on the door. I open it, tip the driver, and take the bag. I pull some plates out of the cabinet and forks out of a drawer, and put them on the card table I'm using as a dining table for now in the kitchen. We both had a rough day; maybe dinner will improve it.

"This is a nice place. You like it here?"

"Yes, definitely colder than Michigan, but not as bad as Helsinki," I joke.

"Michigan? I've never been. I'd like to visit one day. Have to say, though, I'm a Florida native, and I can't imagine not seeing the beach whenever I want."

She puts the puppy on the floor and sits in one of the two

folding chairs at the table. I suddenly realized she is my first official guest since moving in. Cool.

"You're not from New York?"

"No, Dan would love to have me there, but I love the sun and beach too much."

"That explains your tan," I quip, stabbing at my lo Mein noodles.

She puts some noodles on her plate and eats like she hasn't seen food since she left Florida.

"So, what's this you said about the press?" I watch the puppy sniffing and investigating its new surroundings, making a mental note to take her outside to pee as soon as we finish dinner.

"I'm waiting to see if anything leaked, but I think we're okay. The players aren't going to talk. So, who was the girl?" Emily asks.

Whoa. She went from being a woman who rescues and nurtures dogs to Perry Mason peppering me with questions so quickly I have whiplash.

"Her name's Sylvia McDavid. She happens to be our goalie's sister. Meanwhile, she's dating a douchebag who plays for the local university hockey team, where they both attend school. I'm not the asshole I might be getting portrayed as. She pretty much picked me up, and the next morning on her way out, she drops her boyfriend's name. I had no clue he was anybody special. Now, I'm told his dad knows the GM of our team and donates a ton of money to his favorite charity…and there's the rub."

"The GM wants his charity donation, and you end up on the next bus out of town," she finishes my thought as she twists the noodles and delicately pricks a piece of chicken onto the end of her fork before placing the food in her delectable mouth, a mouth I'd love to kiss, and kiss hard –

There I go again. Down, boy.

"Pretty much."

"Well, let me call Dan, see if the GM remembers him, and then discuss with the team how to do damage control. Mainly, we need to make your image shine. Even if it doesn't get out, good PR is never bad."

"You can do that?" I finish my second plate of food and get up to put my dish in the sink. Remembering we brought a dog home, I set a bowl of water on the floor.

"You might want to put a plate or something under that. I'd hate to see that beautiful hardwood floor get ruined. That wood can't be cheap to replace."

"Good idea, thanks," I remark, grabbing a large plate from the cabinet and slipping it under the temporary water bowl.

"I can try. Dan deals with all this stuff, but he picked me to take care of it for some reason. I'm an agent, per se. I'm more of a jack of all trades, primarily one of the agency lawyers, but I've also got a gift for publicity, so I only help the lawyers when they need help behind the scenes. Our big Gold Event is coming up this week, and the others need to be there, especially with Dan laid up, so I'm filling in."

"Speaking of Dan, how is he?"

She half laughs, and half rolls her eyes. "The last text I got said he's laid up with his leg in a cast. That will drive him nuts."

"Yeah, he's pretty energetic for an older guy."

Don't get me wrong, Dan is in great shape, but I'm so young most people look older.

10

———

EMILY

"Oops, sorry, I should have taken her outside," I apologize when the puppy pees on the tiled floor.

Wyatt tosses me a roll of paper towels, and when I bend down to clean it up, I'm teetering in my boots and throw out an arm to stabilize myself. Tipping over would be so embarrassing due to my love of heels.

Wyatt notices my weeble-wobble maneuver and smirks as he sprays the floor with a disinfectant. "I understand you're from Florida, but don't you have a more suitable pair of boots?"

"You know, this thing called winter? I'm not a fan. Why would I need all-weather boots? Only Floridians who take ski trips yearly would have the proper gear for this weather. Plus, this is a quick trip. In and out," I snap my fingers, and the puppy lifts her head and perks her ears up to figure out the sound.

"You're that good, huh?" he jests.

"I've learned from the best marketing companies over the years – trust me, I've seen it all. And about the boot thing? I didn't know I was being sent to an alternate universe of ice, snow, and frozen ponds. Only little kids look cute in snow boots; everyone knows that." I sound like I'm making an argument in court.

"Is that why you still have your coat on?" he asks, watching me wipe up the disinfectant he sprayed.

"Oh, jeez, no wonder I feel warm. Why did you let me leave it on all through dinner?"

"I dunno. I thought you might still be cold. Anyway, make yourself at home. It's not every day I play pond hockey, bring home my agent, who turns out to be a girl, and rescue a puppy amid a blizzard. What started as a boring day has turned into something worth remembering," he laughs as I stand to divest myself of my coat.

"I'm so sorry," I apologize as I hand him my coat and scarf and watch him hang them on a rack by the door. "The puppy was just a spur-of-the-moment thing. Who leaves a puppy to freeze to death anyway?" I try to make excuses for my impromptu rescue. "By the way, are you allowed to have dogs here?"

"No clue. I'm not a fan of reading fine print. That's what I pay Dan and you to do, right? But if it was a problem, I'm sure the concierge would have said something when we came in. I think we're good for now."

I scoop the puppy off the floor, lifting her and cooing, "Who could abandon you?" She's rubbing her cute moist muzzle against my nose, and I let her lick my face. I walk to a white couch, the one real piece of furniture in his living room. I sit, and I put her on my lap. I hope she's done peeing on things and doesn't chew up this leather couch. It's a nice couch in a nice condo. With, um, a nice owner. Shit!

"We should check in on Dan," Wyatt suggests.

"Yeah, I need to see how he's doing." I reach for my purse and rummage through it for my phone. It's one of those bucket purses where everything always falls to the bottom, making it impossible to find anything.

I feel my phone and fish it out triumphantly like I struck gold. Small wins are still worth celebrating.

"I'll call him on speaker." I hit the button that says Dan the Man.

"Dan, the man?" Wyatt mouths to me as we hear Dan pick up.

"Hey, how's it going?" Dan sounds normal, too normal. He's not speaking a mile a minute. I hope that means he's resting.

"Cold! You owe me," I interject.

"I know I do, thanks so much. How's our boy?"

"Fine, he's right here, and I have you on speaker," I reply as Wyatt sits down next to me.

"What's going on? Everything okay?"

"We're calling to check in on you," Wyatt speaks up.

"Hey, Wyatt! Thanks. I'm home now, thank goodness. I needed surgery on my leg, but I'll be okay soon. Damn shame I'll miss the golf tournament this weekend. I was looking forward to seeing the guys and soaking up some rays on the golf course."

"I hear ya, but everything is going well for the event," I reassure him. "And Wyatt here has been played by this girl, but I'll take care of it," I finish.

"Why do people always pick on the new kid?" Wyatt asks, clearly exasperated.

"Because you haven't had a chance to bond with all the guys yet," I answer for Dan.

"Yeah, welcome to the big leagues, kid." Dan's voice catches, and I'm guessing he's in a bit of pain.

"I'll take care of everything here. You get some rest," I say before we wish him well and end the call.

"So, what's the plan?" Wyatt is sitting forward and sounds eager.

It's understandable. I remember what it was like to have my first real job with the public defender's office.

"Well, I've got a call into the GM. I'll work behind the scenes. We need to get you back in the game before the press starts hounding us – no pun intended!" I shake my head at the puppy and put her back on the floor so I can scroll through my phone.

"I'm looking through the socials to see if any more news comes up under the Maine Maulers. All I see are a few posts wondering why you weren't at practice today."

"Damn it! I can't believe Luc's sister is such a shit," Wyatt fumes.

The puppy stops running around and looks back and forth between the two of us before jumping up on my leg for more attention.

"No more negative speculations on social media, so that's a plus," I continue as Wyatt walks into the kitchen and starts doing the dishes. He seems quite domesticated for a bachelor, that's for sure.

"So, how come you don't have a girlfriend?" I ask.

"Oh, so this is my fault?" he fires back. "Like, if I had a steady girlfriend none of this would have happened? That's kind of what-do-you-call-it, victim-blaming, don't you think?"

"No, not necessarily. I mean, I get it."

Finished in the kitchen, Wyatt returns to the living room and the pup who's gnawing on my fingers. It hurts a little because she has sharp teeth.

"Like I said before, Sylvia was all too willing to go home with me. I should have known something was up, but I'm – well, I'm used to it," he finishes a little sheepishly.

"Used to being a jock with girls throwing themselves in your lap?"

He lets out a cute *humph*, ever so slight, that confirms my take on jocks.

"Y-yeah. The problem is, I didn't upgrade who I took home when I upgraded my move to the big leagues," he admits, summing up his mistake in one tidy little sentence.

My eyes widen as I nod in agreement. The guy's more astute than I gave him credit for.

He slumps onto the couch again and pats the puppy's head.

"I screwed up. I'm just over girls. Period. I want to play hockey and do well, you know?" When he looks at me, I see the kid from a small town in Michigan who made it to the pros and is terrified that it might all go down the drain unless I can help him.

I tap his knee. "Cheer up. I'm a whiz at public relations, and we'll get this cleared up. Let me think about it. But it's getting late, and I have to check into my hotel." I stand to go.

"What? You can't take a dog to a hotel!"

"Umm." I look at him, the puppy, and back to him, and reality hits me.

He's right. I can't take the puppy.

I put on a sweet smile and cock my head in a cute, flirty manner that girls only do when they want something.

"Would you mind watching her tonight? I'll be here first thing in the morning, I promise."

"You don't even have a leash," he smirks.

Is that a challenge, I hear?

"Okay, I'll get one, anything else?" I keep my cool. I need him.

"I'm a bachelor with no ties. I'm not taking care of your dog."

Shit, shit, shit!

"Okay, look, I didn't really think this through, but the weather was so bad, and she's so cute," I stammer as I pick up the puppy. As she snuggles into me, I smell her puppy breath.

She's won my heart. I can't give her up. I'm in love with her.

I hold her up to Wyatt with my hand under her butt. "Look, she's so adorable. How can you refuse that cute little puppy face?"

Wyatt takes the dog from me. "Damn it, you owe me, Emily."

"Let's call her Mika. It's got a nice ring to it, don't you think?" I don't give him time to answer. "You take care of her for now, and I'll get you back on the ice this week."

I've been reduced to bargaining and promising something I'm not sure I can deliver, but it sounds good. It also buys me time to think clearly because staring at him in his long-sleeved shirt, snug across his chest and biceps, has my head spinning and is making me realize I have to bolt out of here ASAP.

He's too young for me. I can't possibly go out with a man that's nine whole years younger than me and a client besides. But damn, he's rocking his fitted jeans. This little mess with Sylvia is just a tiny piece of sand in the hourglass of his life. I hope he can understand that.

"Look, you didn't get where you are by giving up hope, don't give up now," I try to reassure him.

I know what it's like to feel alone in a new place, surrounded by others who all know more than you at the time. God knows I made my share of mistakes along the way, we all have.

At least he was in the dating game, well, maybe not dating, but he was putting himself out there, which is more than I can say for myself.

I can't take my eyes off him holding the cute puppy. She looks so small against his broad chest, and I melt. He's that sexy.

"You know when you name a dog, you jinx yourself, right?"

"What do you mean?" I look inquisitively into his large brown eyes and note a hint of a smile on his kissable lips.

"If you name a dog, you're not giving it up," he says flatly as he cuddles her in one large arm and tickles her ears.

"Is that a rule…"

"No, science," he interrupts and flashes me a smile I find is both confident and deadly. "So, I'll watch the pup at night, but you'd better be here first thing in the morning because I don't do mornings. And I can't have her peeing all over the place."

I like how he's taking control of the situation even though I'm the one who created it.

"Okay." I pick up my purse and phone. "Then it's a deal. I'll make some calls and see you first thing in the morning."

"Great," he says, walking me to the door, where I retrieve my coat and scarf, bracing myself for the lower temperatures now that the sun has gone down.

"Thank you."

"No problem." I hope he means it as the door closes, and I'm left to head to my empty hotel room.

The day was strange, but the company and the food were good. The fact that he can clean up the kitchen himself is pretty amazing.

I pass the empty concierge desk and smile. He must have left hours ago. I push the heavy glass doors open and get blasted with the cold air that fills my lungs and takes my breath away.

I miss Mika already and decide to find a store to get her a collar. All dogs like collars. It means they have a home.

11

WYATT

As soon as Emily leaves to go to her hotel, it's as if the room gets colder, even though there isn't a draft. Why does she have to be so damn hot? I gave her a hard time about the boots, but I must admit, they look good on her. I wonder how many more pairs of boots and heels she has in her collection.

I'm at her mercy regarding my future in hockey, so I have to make sure that we don't cross professional boundaries. The last thing she needs is to be entangled in my personal life. She's here to fix it, not be a part of it.

Mika sits and stares up at me.

"What do you want?" I ask her as if she will answer me.

She whines.

I chuckle.

"I know, I miss her too, but we need to cope. Let's go outside," I suggest. I grab my jacket off the coat rack while Mika nips at my heels.

I pick her up, carry her outside, and watch as she bounces about gleefully before peeing.

"Good girl." I praise her after I pick her up. "You are one lucky puppy, you know." I carry her back to the elevator.

Back in my condo, I looked around for a ball for her to play with. No such luck, so a hockey puck it is. Five minutes later, the puck is dotted with tiny impressions from her puppy teeth.

I'll be damned.

I decided to call my old hockey buddy from Juniors. We were on the same team for two years, and I've been meaning to return his text from yesterday informing me that he made it onto a minor league team in Toronto.

"Tristan! What's up, man? Geez, it's so good to hear from you. Congrats on making the team in Toronto," I lean back on the couch, engaging the footrest with the push of a button and kicking off my sneakers. I really gotta get some more furniture to go with this couch.

"It's only the minors," he protests.

"Hey, it's still a move up, be positive. How have the last few weeks been, anyway?"

"So far, it's been great. The team's management has been here a long time, and the low turnover rate makes me feel like they are a good organization to work for," he adds.

"Well, that's great. I'm not so sure about mine," I say, hoping he'll honor the bro code of not repeating anything.

It's not something I worry about. The hockey world is similar to a fraternity with its code of conduct and layers of protective silence. We don't have a secret handshake, but there is constant boys-being-boys hazing, that's for sure.

"What is this I hear about you missing a game?"

"It was just a practice."

"You okay?"

"Yeah, more political than anything. And here I thought the hardest part of joining a new team would be stepping up my game and getting acclimated to a new city."

I look for Mika and see her scampering across the slick wood floor to chase the rolling puck.

"It'll all blow over soon." I have no doubt that Emily can fix it. I'll believe her until I don't, and that will bring a whole set of trust issues.

Issues I'm not ready to deal with or even contemplate at this point in time.

"Cold as fuck, ya know?"

"Tell me about it." I put him on speaker while we look at our weather apps and compared the temperatures in our respective cities. We're always making things a competition.

"Damn, I'm colder than you, dude. I don't want to hear about the fact that you guys are on a warming trend. It's still below zero here some nights. That's a real zero, you know, zero Fahrenheit, not the fake zero Celsius you have in Canada. What is that, like 32?"

He chuckles. "Geez. Lucky you."

"Tell me about it, man. It sucks. But the pond hockey was amazing. In fact, I hope to get back out there. I tried to remain anonymous, but then my agent showed up and totally blew my cover."

"Oh no, what did you do?" He chuckles again, getting a kick out of my drama.

"I had to come clean. They were nice guys, and I'd love to go back and play with them again. Dude, it's so—quiet out here. If you break down on the road, forget it. I haven't seen a moose yet, but I heard they can be super dangerous."

"Ha, sounds like Maine is a lot like Alaska minus the six months of darkness thing," he chips in without missing a beat.

"True, so what else is going on?"

"Nothing much. The girls here like American accents, but I haven't met many yet. I've only been up here two weeks. My birthday is coming up, though."

"That's right, you'll be legal to drink there. Their drinking age is 19, right?"

"Yeah! I'm stoked. Gotta find something fun to do. Any ideas?"

"No clue, man. I'm still getting used to the new guys here myself, it all feels a bit weird, y'know?"

"Yeah, but at least you don't have to try and navigate a huge metropolitan city like this."

"I'm kinda digging this place. I'll take a city with less than 200,000 people any day. I can't imagine living where you are."

"The public transportation system in Toronto is great, with subways and plenty of buses. Bike lanes right in the center of the city, too. That'll be cool come summer."

This makes sense since I've heard that Canadians are very much into protecting the environment. Maybe it's easier because there are fewer people compared to the United States.

"I'm just trying to adjust to being the new guy in town and putting down some roots, you know? The Mustang is in storage for the winter. I can't drive it on the roads, so I'm using my old Tahoe."

"Smart, yeah, ya gotta do that. So, pond hockey, huh? How was that? I haven't played in so long."

"It's neat y'know, not a formal setup at all like some of the places we've played. I had to get the rust off, but I got into the swing of it quickly. Basically, I nailed it."

"Ha! Modest as ever, Wyatt. I'll bet you showed them how it's done."

Mika is sitting next to the couch, staring at me when she debuts her first bark. I think she's jealous that I'm on the phone and not paying attention to her.

"Whoa, dude, was that a dog?"

"Yeah, long story. I mean, short, but strange. I have a female attorney. She's here to run my public relations. She is filling in for my agent. Crazy as it sounds, she found this puppy on our way back from the hockey game at the pond."

"Wait. Back up. How long has she been there? You hitting that?"

"Nope, I might be young, but I know better than to mix business with my personal life. Besides, it's just not good timing. I'm taking a break from girls. I have plenty of time to jump back into the dating pool after I get into my routine here."

"I hear ya, not a bad plan. What kind of dog, anyway?"

"Shepherd, puppy. Someone dumped her on the side of the road in a blizzard."

"That's terrible. Well, it's a good thing you guys found it. What are you going to do when you're on the road?"

"It's not mine. It's Emily's."

"Emily, huh?"

"My attorney, PR lady, whatever. I can't take care of a dog. Are you nuts? No, it will go back to Miami with Emily. It's just staying here while she's in a hotel."

"Sounds to me like you're already in two relationships," he teases.

"Hum, well, let's catch up again before your birthday. I gotta go," I add as Mika lets out another yip, trying to find her voice. I don't want the neighbors to be disturbed, and I don't need any other issues.

"Later, man." We hang up.

I sit on the floor to give Mika some tummy rubs and decide it's time to feed her again. We had dogs growing up, but they were outside most of the time. I recall we fed them twice a day, but they burned tons of calories running around.

My phone dings.

I reach to get it off the coffee table. It's Emily.

How's Mika doing?

Great.

I got her a leash.

Nice.

Then a picture of a fuchsia collar pops up on my phone.

I chuckle. If I know Emily, she'll have a huge stash of dog stuff tomorrow- a real Santa Claus in February.

After I feed Mika and take her out again, I play some video games.

Then I text Alexandre, my best link to what's going on with the team.

He video calls me. "Practice went well. Things are cooling down. I met your sexy agent today. Zut alors."

"What the hell is that?" I can only say 'please' and 'thank you' in French.

"It means holy shit! She's fucking hot man!"

Oh, boy, I wish that hadn't happened because it's going to be locker-room talk now. Whether we're bonking each other or not, the guys will give me a hard time since the one-night stand with Sylvia has branded me a Casanova.

"Don't get ahead of yourself, man. I'm still swearing off women. Besides, Emily appears unapproachable. She probably has a boyfriend, I don't know. I'm sure she has better offers than me. I'm not stupid enough to do my public relations rep."

"Ha, tell yourself what you want, but your street cred just went up. You're NHL now, remember."

"It doesn't feel like it unless I'm in the game."

"It will blow over, don't worry. I've been around, I know things."

We talk nonsense for a few minutes before hanging up. I turn on an old *Fast and Furious* movie to pass the time while Mika curls up in my lap. The puppy stage is so magical. I can understand Emily being sucked in by Mika's hazel eyes and cute wet nose.

I'm wondering what's going to happen to my pristine condo with its white walls and leather couch after she's here a few days. Maybe it's just as well I haven't invested in furniture yet.

I get another text from Emily and fill her in on Mika.

Before we sign off, I remind her: *Tomorrow, early.*

I'm on it.

I smile at how cute she is when she gives me attitude, and I wonder if she has some brothers or played sports. She seems to have a smart head on her shoulders and enough in the tank to take on anyone at any time.

Mika and I have a water and pee break and then head to bed. She follows me into the bedroom, and I lift her up onto the bed with me. What the hell, why not? It's not like we got her a dog bed today.

I crawl into bed wearing only PJ bottoms and hope this pup sleeps through the night. It's not like I have early plans, but still, I'm used to being alone most of the time.

I lie on my side and watch Mika walk around the bed, trying to figure out where she should curl up. She finds a spot against my back, and before long, I hear her soft breathing as she falls asleep. Meanwhile, I'm still wide awake.

I feel better now that Emily is here to handle things. It's still unclear how she plans to go about resurrecting my reputation.

She sure looked cute stomping through the snow at the lake today, even with her hair blowing in the wind and her nose red from the cold. The coat she's wearing isn't warm enough for this kind of cold. I could tell she wasn't leaving until she found me, so I had to give myself up, which was fine. I think the guys I met today at the lake were nice, and hopefully, I made some new friends.

I grab my phone, checking the hockey sites Emily watches for any further fallout from the Sylvia situation. All I can see is one post from an ex-high school girlfriend saying I'm a great boyfriend and that we only broke up because we couldn't make the long-distance relationship work.

I smile. Yeah, we were young. I'm thankful that my first girl-friend has nice things to say and is willing to share them in a public forum. I can use the support right now. Now I'm wondering what the press is up to. What are they digging for? Since when is it such a slow news day that they are following me rather than getting ready for the Junior tournaments that are coming up soon?

And then I remember stuff that was important to me before I made it here. Now, I need to shift my focus to the pros.

I wish they'd move on to the next hot rookie or the goalie who had his sixth shutout in a row or something. That should be filling the airwaves, not my dirty laundry.

I turn over. Mika snuggles behind my knees. I wonder if Emily has a boyfriend in Miami. I'm sure she does. I'm not sure how I would feel if I found out she was involved with someone.

Then I remind myself that I'm resolved to stay unattached. Girls are trouble, and she has all the makings of the kind of girl you marry. She's not a one-nighter kind of girl. She's the kind of girl you take home to mom. That alone should take her off my radar. But I can't get her out of my mind.

12

EMILY

By the time I reach my hotel room, I'm convinced it's only my dirty clothes holding me up. Between the travel, the puppy, and Wyatt, I am physically and mentally exhausted.

Without bothering to unpack, I lie on the bed with my boots still on. It would be so easy to close my eyes and sleep, but I need a shower. The more I think about it, the better it sounds.

I sit up, unzip my boots, and rub my tired feet before walking to the bathroom. I flip the light switch, and a warming lamp starts to glow. Jackpot! Now I can shower without feeling a chill when I towel off. I had forgotten about those, as it's been so long since I was anywhere cold.

When I was at Wyatt's place, I noticed he had a sauna. Gee, what a brilliant idea – especially during the cold winters here.

As I peel off my clothes, I hear my phone playing the theme song from *Gilmore Girls,* which means it's a text from Mom. She's checking in on me. I text her back that I'm fine but tired and going to bed.

It's nice of her to remember I'm out of town.

Then I hear a flow arts theme, and it's Natalie. I forgot she had texted earlier when I was too busy with Mika to answer. I called her this morning after I boarded the plane. I text her to say I'm getting in the shower and will call in a few minutes.

Looking in the mirror, my hair looks flat from the lack of humidity, and I hope washing it will fix it. I step into the warm shower and reach for the hotel's shampoo as the water cascades over me.

As I lather my hair, my mind wanders to Wyatt and his friendly, warm smile. I've always found that when an athlete is trying to make an impression, they can drop the frat guy façade and be as charming as a prince. Wyatt's genuine smile and zippy banter made him good company today. I'm tired of men telling me what I want to hear and making assumptions before they even know me.

And then seeing him hold the puppy in the crook of his arm as I was leaving melted my heart. Poor little Mika, cute as a button, but her owners didn't want her. I hate to think anyone would be so cruel as to leave her there all alone in a blizzard. Some people shouldn't be allowed to have dogs.

After the shower and with a towel wrapped over my head, I put on my thin cotton PJs and crank up the heat in the room. I miss Mika and wish she was here to snuggle. Until today, I didn't realize how much I missed having a dog.

Wyatt's right; I won't be able to give her up. He might be young, but he's good at reading me.

I grab a bottle of water and crawl into bed, fluffing the pillows behind me to support my back and call Natalie. The central heat is making my throat dry, so I sip the water to clear it.

"Hey girl, how are you?"

"Great, you?"

"Eventful day, I thought Wyatt's case was a big deal, but it's just a girl using him to get even with her boyfriend. It's all so juvenile."

"Unbelievable. So, what is Wyatt like? I Googled him today. He's hot," she gushes.

"He is," I reply warmly. I couldn't agree more. In fact, if this hockey thing doesn't pan out, I'll bet he could always be an underwear model for Calvin Klein. Not that I've pictured him barechested in just his underwear. Oh, who am I kidding? Of course, I have.

"So, what's he like?"

"Sweet, actually. As expected, a bit freaked out, as any new player on a team would be in this situation."

"Well, things are gearing up here for the golf tournament. The office was busy today with guys stopping by."

"I bet…oh, fun fact—I rescued a German Shepherd puppy today!"

"What? How did you manage to do that in your first twelve hours away from home?"

"I was driving behind Wyatt heading back from the hockey pond –oh yeah, that's where I finally found him, but that's another story. That's when I saw something small and dark moving in a field covered with snow. It's good that I was taking in the scenery and paying attention; otherwise, I would have driven right past her. She didn't look like a bunny or any other critter that would normally be out this time of year, so I pulled over to check it out. I decided to call her Mika."

"Oh, no! You named her? I predict you're coming home with that dog. Are you even allowed dogs where you live?"

"Yes, small ones, I think."

"Girl, that's going to be a large dog."

"I know."

"What is your plan to get Wyatt some good PR?'

"Always a charity event, and if there isn't one, I guess I'll have to create it. I'll know more tomorrow after talking to people with the Maulers. Maybe they already have an event that we can use to benefit. At first I thought I'd be able to get in and out quickly, but now it looks like need to stay a bit longer. Not too much longer, I hope. It's fucking cold."

"Oh, poor you. I know how you hate that. Well, keep me posted. I know you've totally got this, You're amazing at PR, and I'll help you with whatever I can."

"I appreciate that," I reply before we say good night.

I text Wyatt to see how my baby is doing. She's such a sweet puppy. I feel bad dumping her on Wyatt, but what else can I do? Most hotels don't allow pets, leading to another issue: I'll have to be at Wyatt's every day.

That means I'll have to ignore how he makes my body tingle when he stands next to me. I need to keep it professional. I toss and turn, trying to think of things I might be able to do for Wyatt to save this situation.

Finally, I sit up, pull my laptop out of its bag, and start searching for events in the area. There has to be something these people do to keep occupied in the long winter months, stuff that occurs outside their homes. There's more to Maine than Lobster rolls, I hope.

I've lived in Florida my entire life, and I'm clueless about what people up here do besides skiing and snowboarding. I never fell in love with skiing, preferring to hang out in the ski lodge when I would join Dan in Colorado to schmooze the jet set and famous athletes, preferably ones looking for new representation.

Too tired to see straight, I glance at my fitness watch - midnight.

Crap, I have to be at Wyatt's early before Mika disturbs him. It's bad enough that I crashed his pad yesterday, I don't want the puppy chewing the place up and peeing on everything. I log off my laptop.

I want to look my best tomorrow. I need sleep. I roll over and close my eyes, but I see Wyatt, not Mika, in my dreams.

My alarm goes off, and I sit up, trying to remember where I am and why it is so effing cold. Ah, yes, Maine. With no time to waste, I throw back the covers and make coffee using the small drip machine in my room. I dress as warmly as possible and pull on the same boots. I might need more shoes if I stay here much longer.

I grab my coat and purse and swing by the complimentary breakfast in the lobby to grab a croissant and another cup of coffee on my way to my rental car.

I start the car and turn up the heat. It's so cold I can see my breath swirling and dancing before it disappears. My fingers are freezing, so I wrap them around the hot cup of coffee and wait for the car and myself to warm up.

Fifteen minutes later, I'm parking at Wyatt's, and when I open the car door, the car reminds me I have things in the back seat. What the - oh yes, puppy stuff. I grab the bag and quickly walk through below-zero temps while shoving my scarf into my trench coat.

"Morning, miss," the concierge greets me, and I can feel his eyes on me as I head to the elevator.

I knock on Wyatt's door and turn the knob to see if he left it open for me. Nope.

I knock louder.

"Coming," he calls, and I hear the lock slide.

"Morning," he says. He's wearing PJ bottoms; all I can see is his bare muscular chest, the size of Maine itself.

I'm flustered and divert my eyes to Mika, who leaps onto my leg, clearly happy to see me.

"Good morning, how was she?"

"Aside from pee breaks at two and four a.m., pretty good," and he runs his bear paw-sized hand through his thick hair. "Coffee," he remarks in the middle of a yawn.

"Twice in the night, she woke you up? Shit, I'm so sorry." I pick up Mika and rub my cheek against her soft puppy fur. "I bet you need to go out, don't you?" I ask her, dropping the shopping bag containing her collar, leash, and toys on the floor.

I lay my purse on the kitchen counter and go about trying to get the collar on her while she's busy wiggling and nipping at it.

"Here." Wyatt takes over, slips the collar over her head, and adjusts it properly.

"Oh wow, thanks, you've had dogs before?"

"Yep, it's hard having one when I'm on the road, so I thought it would be one of those in-the-foreseeable-future things. "Yeah, I hear ya." I look at Mika. "So, you ready to go outside?"

She starts to sit, then gets up again and lets out a Yip.

I attach her leash and walk her to the door. Wyatt hands me a plastic bag, "I'm sure we have a pick-up-after-your-dog policy."

"Good point. Thanks."

Mika is clearly settling into her temporary home and knows her way around now. We have a brief walk, she piddles and poops, and then we return to the condo.

When I enter, I smell a delicious aroma.

"Is that a cappuccino?" I ask, my mouth watering.

"Yep, this machine does everything. You want one?" he asks, noticing me eyeing his cup.

"Sure. Any chance there's some chocolate to go in that?"

He holds up a bottle of chocolate syrup. "Good enough?"

"Oh, yeah," I smile. What girl wouldn't, with such a specimen standing before her? And making her coffee for bonus points?

I busy myself with the bag of dog toys and place them on the floor, trying to entice Mika to try one.

"So, I need to make some calls. Are you going back to sleep?"

"Just because I'm awake doesn't make me an early morning person. I like lazy mornings before I get motivated to do what needs to be done."

"Oh, right. Well, I have to make some calls and set up some appointments. I'll try to be as quiet as I can."

"Great. Go ahead. Don't mind me." He pushes a button on the machine, and after a minute of noise, he hands me a hot cup of cappuccino with chocolate in it.

We hold eye contact longer than normal after he gives it to me.

To break the awkward silence, I say, "Thanks for watching Mika last night."

"She kept me warm. I should be thanking you."

For a second, I'm jealous of Mika.

I sip from my cup and watch him walk away, that bubble butt snug against his pajama pants. My one big weakness is a cute ass.

I inhale deeply. Work, right? How can I be expected to get anything done when it's just the two of us in his condo, and he's walking around with next to nothing on?

I set up shop at his kitchen table and ran down the list of names and numbers Dan texted me this morning. He made some calls for me, and I'm waiting for some more to come in as I roll around on the floor with Mika.

13

WYATT

Just because I'm awake in the morning doesn't mean I like to get out of bed, especially when the weather is this cold. But today, I got up because I couldn't wait to see Emily when she got here this morning – not that she needs to know that. Emily arrives early, as promised, and looks refreshed and somehow younger than she did yesterday. She seems relaxed and comfortable in an oversized sweater dress with black leggings and boots. Her long, thick hair is up in a messy bun that I'm tempted to undo to run my fingers through.

When she returns from taking Mika outside, I make her a cappuccino and head back to my room, leaving her to focus on her work.

"Hey Wyatt, what do you think about a Celebrity Skate to raise money for hockey leagues for the 18 and under kids?" she hollers across the condo, her words echoing off the bare tiled floors.

"That sounds awesome, but you have to have some big names to pull that off. Is Keanu Reeves in town?" I holler back, trying to make my point and make it funny at the same time.

"Ha ha, I agree. But instead of a game with players from two different teams, we can do a skating event with the top four players on your team. We'll bill you as the 'hottest new addition.' They are good buzzwords. We'll charge admission, put it out to the boosters, and get more donations as well."

"Sure," I agree, standing in the doorway to my room and tossing back what's left of my coffee. "That should work. It's easy since the whole team is in town anyway."

"Exactly," she replies, chewing on the end of her purple ink pen. It must be a nervous habit. Everyone has a few.

"Anything else?" I ask, knowing full well I'm still walking around half-dressed. I enjoy that it's getting harder for her to take her eyes off my broad shoulders and rock-hard abs.

"Hmm, let me run it up the chain of command," she replies, finally tearing her eyes off my six-pack to look over the notes she's made in her travel-size book.

"What?" I would love to know what she's really thinking.

"Oh, sorry, I'm just lost in thoughts, that's all."

"Fair enough." I tap the door frame before I walk out to the common area. Maybe she wants to brainstorm.

"I'll call Dan, run it by him, and get players' names. We'll coordinate with the PR staff for the team to put something together. They'll know who to use for this event."

"Wait, William Barber is the father of that jerk, Cole Barber, right?" I ask.

"Yeah, why?" she asks, taking the pen out of her mouth.

"Well, he's a huge corporate sponsor, oil business. He has advertising everywhere when you go to the arena," I inform her. "Dunno if he's gonna want to sponsor that."

"Oh." Emily leans forward, putting her forehead on the table in momentary defeat. I watch a few strands of hair fall out of her messy bun or chignon. I don't even know if there's a difference between the two. When she looks up, the loose strands frame her face. She takes my breath away. I make a tiny cough to cover it up as I am about to choke on my own saliva or drool.

She sits up again. "Well, Wyatt, you're not the headliner, no offense, so we just can't wave your name in front of him. Easy. If we can get him to sponsor the event with the team's owner, and the GM's approval, that should put everything to bed lickety-split."

She excitedly dials her phone, and I hear Dan on speaker as she brings him up to date on the situation.

"Yikes. Okay. Well, the Barber issue adds a wrinkle to the plan for sure, but I'm sure you will find a way to make it happen," Dan says confidently.

"Okay, I have your numbers, and I'll try to set up a meeting now that we have a plan. It's for a good cause. This could be fun," Emily finishes. I can see she's getting a second wind now that Dan is in the loop.

"I'll call the few sponsors I know and see what I can do," Dan replies.

"We need backpacks and some team giveaways since we'll be charging for the kids to skate with the players, too."

"There will be t-shirts left over from other events, maybe summer leagues the team sponsored," Dan suggests.

"Perfect. I'll look into it."

I take advantage of their phone call to play with Mika before taking her outside again. She'll outgrow the collar in a few months but looks cute in that bright, hot pink.

Emily hangs up from talking to Dan and asks me, "So, do you know your guy downstairs, the one who sits at the desk in the lobby?"

"No more than you. I haven't been here that long. Why?"

"Just wondering. I'm not used to having a concierge, I guess."

"I think his name is Ted. Ted Mackey. I can call him if I need stuff or have problems in the building."

"Yeah, nice service," she adds, but something seems to be bothering her.

"Mackey didn't do anything to you, did he?"

"No." She quickly brushes it aside like the stray piece of hair she just tucked behind her ear.

"Good, if someone does, tell me." I suddenly feel protective of her.

Mika plays with a squeaky ball, and I catch Emily smiling at the pup, having fun with her new toys.

"What?" she asks when she catches me watching her and shaking my head.

"I knew you'd go overboard."

"Hey, a lot of toys for a puppy is a good thing," she rattles on about her spending spree at the pet store.

"It is," I concede. But I should know better than to put a stamp of approval on overspending, no matter how much money she has. Then again, she's not my girlfriend. I'm supposed to be impartial and remain unattached.

"Hungry for lunch?" I ask, changing the subject and pushing down the beginnings of emotional attachment that is welling up in me. Puppies do that.

"Yes, actually. These hotels are trying to kill me with carbs. Carbs that go straight from my lips to my hips." She gently slaps her butt in a cute manner. She has a sense of humor.

"Well, if you ask me, I don't see it, but then again, I don't see much with you wearing oversized sweaters and that big coat that's not warm enough for our winter."

"This was probably the style the last time I needed cold-weather clothing," she chuckles. "Don't judge my clothes." And she strikes a pose with her hands on her hips and her lower lip sticking out in a cute little pout.

Her face turns serious, and I wonder if I offended her somehow but before I inquire, she continues to think out loud.

"I'll need different clothing if we do this event. I didn't think to pack anything other than one suit."

"Wear it twice, What's the big deal?"

"Ha, obviously, you aren't used to representing your team in the big leagues. I know you dress up for games, but I have to look good when I'm around clients, which comes with a large price tag."

"I don't think you need a whole new wardrobe, nothing that a nice pair of heels and miniskirt can't fix." I grin.

"That's for after hours, and you know it," she teases me back, giving me the side eye to keep me in check. "I'm thinking we can hold one of those meet-the-players sip-and-see events. Yes, that's all we need," she says, almost to herself, and her smile tells me she's pleased with her solution.

I watch her as she writes in her notebook. Sunlight beams through the living room windows, picks up the contrasting colors in her hair, and caresses her high cheekbones with a warm glow. The tendrils of blonde hair that have escaped her messy bun give her a sexy vixen vibe. She may not realize it, but she's sucking me in without even trying.

"It's time I got dressed, so give me a few, and we'll figure lunch out," I suggest, realizing that I've been so distracted with her here that I haven't even showered yet.

"Sounds good. I'll just finish up my calls, then it's wait and see."

"Great." I slip into my room.

I shuck off my clothes and try to ignore the boner I have. Damn, she's hot—definitely time for a cold shower.

I have to be careful. Emily can easily coax flames out of the embers of attraction I'm fighting to ignore. Damn, I need to get the stats on her.

I rub one out in the shower, but it's a short-term fix to a long-term issue. As in, an issue of the heart like 'when am I going to settle down with someone '- kind of issue.

It's not for lack of trying, but I've never met anyone who gives me the electricity shooting through my body feeling I get when I'm around Emily.

Seeing her with the puppy yesterday really sealed the deal. Who can resist a puppy anyway? I like that she picked the dog up when she found it. I like that she's responsible. Whether she keeps it or finds it a home is immaterial.

I pull on my Lucky jeans and a long-sleeved collared shirt to step up my game from my usual sweatshirt or t-shirt. I'm having lunch with a gorgeous woman, after all. The fact that she probably dates attorneys and athletes who are older than me plays with my mind. She probably has guys lined up for dinner dates to the best restaurants and a jet to take them there as well.

My overthinking simmers down by the time I return back to the living room, where I find Emily on the floor giggling with Mika. She looks so normal, surely I'm missing something, but I shrug it off and join them for puppy playtime.

"We have a game tonight, but I'll have to sit in the stands." I try not to sound too disappointed as I pet Mika.

"Yeah, well, hopefully it's just this game."

I appreciate her being supportive, and her confidence makes me feel better.

Emily's phone rings, and she jumps up to grab it off the table with the pup nipping at her heels.

"Yes, yes, that would be great. Tomorrow at ten o'clock."

She hangs up.

"What was that?"

"I have a meeting tomorrow with the public relations team, and I think you should come with me to make a good impression."

"Of course." I stand and brush off the dog hair.

"Great." She sweeps tendrils of hair up off her long neck and tucks it back in her bun. Oh, how I'd love to nibble on that delectable neck.

"Do you want anything else? Or should we just go grab some grub?"

"Grabbing grub? That's romantic." She lets a giggle slip out.

I find it adorable.

She glances at me again, and our eyes meet in a pregnant pause. I quickly avert my eyes and grab my coat so we can get out of here. She's smoking hot, but I can't come off like a kid who chases skirts more than his hockey puck.

"I don't know many places around here. There's a family diner around the corner."

"Maybe you should speak to the concierge downstairs. He probably knows every good joint in town," she suggests as she takes her coat from me. I help her slide it on.

I shrug my shoulders as I grab my quilted vest. "You're right, we'll ask him for a good place. Whatever you want."

"My treat," she smiles as she picks up her purse and phone. She pats Mika on the head. "You be a good girl."

Mika gets excited and follows on her heels as she makes her way to the door. I follow on her heels, too, enjoying the sway of her hips.

We start down the hall. "So, you haven't told me much about yourself," I begin, intent on finding out more about her.

"Not much to know. I'm pretty simple. I work, and spend Sunday at the beach. Now, I'll have little Mika to keep me company when I'm home. She's going to be big for my tiny place."

"I imagine rent is expensive there."

"Where isn't it?"

We stop off at Mackey's desk, and I introduce Emily.

"Hi Ted, this is Emily, my agent, and we're looking for a good place to eat lunch. Do you have any recommendations?"

"What kind of food?"

"How about Italian? Can't go wrong there."

"Sure, it's called Luna's Italian Restaurant, and it's about five minutes from here," Mackey says.

Emily looks it up on her phone. "Got it. And we won't need a reservation?"

"Not for lunch, I wouldn't think," replies Ted. "Dinner during the weekend, maybe."

"Great, thanks," I say, opening the door for Emily to exit ahead of me. As I catch up and walk beside her, she slides on the icy concrete sidewalk and grabs my arm to steady herself.

"Oh my God," she exclaims, recovering from nearly falling. "Do you mind if I hang onto your arm?"

"Not at all." I make sure to flex my bicep while getting her safely to my vehicle. It's a different kind of torture, knowing she's off-limits.

She's our navigator to the restaurant, and I like that she's present in every moment we spend together. She doesn't spend all her time with her nose in her phone like girls my age.

"Stay where you are. I'm walking you in." I order her while flashing my trademark boyish grin. I unfasten my seatbelt before hustling around to open her door.

"Thank you," she murmurs, sliding her hand in mine as I help her to the ground, and then she's holding onto my bicep while walking to the establishment.

Once inside Luna's, we're greeted with the warmth of the pizza oven and the smell of freshly baked garlic knots.

"Oh, boy, this place smells incredible," she says, dropping my arm.

I hoped she'd keep it there because her touch makes my body tingle.

14

EMILY

How does he expect me to finish any work when I can't get my eyes off his navel? And one that is perfect, by the way. He doesn't have much chest hair or body fat so I can see the cuts of his physique clearly. I'd love to run my fingers over his body, his skin looks so smooth. I find it strange that his skin is so white, but I guess that's how it is living and working in cold climates.

I'm sitting at the large island in his kitchen, ironing out the fundraising events. He catches me staring at his chest and abs as he walks around the condo wearing only jogging pants.

Shit.

Focus, focus, focus.

"At tonight's game, you will have to sit behind your team in the stands, right?" I'm not sure what the etiquette is for this situation.

"Yeah, I can dress casually for this. You want to join me for dinner and the game?"

"Is it allowed?"

"I'm sitting next to others. Besides, you're my representative."

He's right. I am doing the work of an agent, and now I'm in the spotlight, much more than I ever bargained for, but as long as he's with me, I don't mind. I never thought about being with a public figure before, even though I always deal with them. I prefer to be the person behind the scenes. I'm exposed to less public criticism if I stay safely tucked behind my desk.

And if I stay hidden, my heart will not get broken.

"I guess so," I agree, unable to keep the excitement from my voice.

AT THE RESTAURANT, we order a bottle of white wine to go with our food and discuss the options for appetizers and entrees.

"Oh yeah, seafood!" I'm about to com in my pants at all the choices on the menu when I remember we're in Maine, and they have lobsters and oysters. "Oysters from Florida just aren't the same as the ones off the coast of Maine, and if they're Boston oysters, they have the most brine, in my opinion. But Canadian oysters are awesome, too."

"Hmm, never gave it much thought before. Maybe we need to get an appetizer of assorted oysters so we can compare."

I emphatically reply, "Let's! This will be fun. Do you eat them straight or with stuff on them?"

"I usually decide when I see them. You?"

"I'm naked with lemon or maybe a touch of horseradish."

"I see you aren't shy," he teases me.

"Nope, well, once in a while maybe." I lean forward, put an elbow on the table, and rest my chin on my palm. When I look across the table, Wyatt is giving me a mischievous grin.

I feel my face blush. Keep it together, girl. "Well, I guess that's a conversation for another day," I say, leaning back again.

I give him an out, but he doesn't take it. "Yes, I look forward to those conversations. Tell me more about yourself, Miss Emily," he says while sipping his wine.

"Short answer, two siblings, no daddy issues, I have a job, a best friend, and I've been single for over a year."

"Why?"

"Why are you? It's hard. I think I just got to the point I needed a break."

"I get that," he says, nodding.

"You do? But you're so young, surely you can't be soured on love."

"Not love, just women. How do you know who to trust?" And just like that, our conversation turns serious.

"You don't, really. None of us do. We can't read each other's minds. Everyone has free will, which means the situation can go either way."

"True." He thinks for a moment, then switches topics. "It's gonna suck to sit in the stands tonight."

"Yeah, but let's hope it's for the last time," I reply with a reassuring smile.

The lunch crowd starts to pour in, and the volume in the restaurant gradually increases as the clatter of plates picks up, and everyone talks louder to be heard.

Wyatt orders our oysters. I have no clue what I want to eat for lunch. I'm usually not so indecisive. Is he affecting my ability to concentrate?

"I don't want too much food to eat. What are you having? A meatball sub doesn't exactly go with oysters." I play with the ends of my hair that have escaped my messy bun.

I fix my hair, taking the clip out and letting it down for a moment before sweeping it into another updo.

"You're so pretty, Emily, do you know that?"

I can't look at him. Compliments have always made me uncomfortable. Instead, I stare at my glass of wine and mumble, "Thanks."

"Look at me," he says and places a finger under my chin to lift my face so our eyes can meet.

"I'm not used to that," I stammer as I gaze at his kissable lips. I wonder how they would feel… warm, inviting, addicting.

I'm feeling a pang of emptiness in my stomach that's not a hunger for food, but for affection, for love, and to receive them both from a man who treats me well. Emotions like these are dangerous, and the scary part is that they make me… vulnerable.

"I'm not used to letting anyone in. I'm afraid."

"Of what?"

"Of being hurt, used. It's tough…now that I'm older, the guys my age are either married or confirmed bachelors. I have to make sure my date isn't hiding a wedding ring. It's just become so… contrived, unappealing, and stressful."

"You're preaching to the choir. We are here because of Sylvia. Men get burned too, you know."

"Right." I nod and feel I might actually crack a smile at any minute. "Yeah, your situation is a real-life clusterfuck, I'll give you that."

He lets out a hearty laugh as he drinks from his wine glass.

I reach for mine, take a sip of the light white, and let it gently roll down my throat. The flavor is perfect, and I run the tip of my tongue over my lower lip as if to taste the wine again and imagine his lips on mine.

"Thanks, I'm an overachiever," he chuckles. His cute grin turns me inside out. I take another sip of wine and sneak a peek at his profile as he watches for our waitress to bring another basket of warm bread.

I can't deny I'm attracted to him. I know there's an age difference, but he seems older than nineteen. All this time, I've been thinking of him as a kid, but he's mature, having traveled around Europe and been away from home for years.

Again, I pump the brakes on my runaway-train thoughts. There's no way I can get involved with my client, and I certainly can't give into temptation.

Our waitress appears with the bread, and I decide on the stuffed shells with a side salad. No sooner is Wyatt done ordering when another waitress swings by our table with the raw oysters. Before leaving, she points out there are two each from Maine, Boston, and Canada.

"These look great," I say, shaking my napkin and placing it in my lap.

"Ladies first," Wyatt announces as he puts a small plate in front of him, "I say let's work from the south to the north."

"Okay, so that means we're eating the Boston oysters first. They'll be the briniest."

"Yep."

"Gentlemen, start your engines." I'm excited as I take the tiny fork and the oyster, add a dash of horseradish, and then flip it down my throat.

"Whoa, you're a freaking pro at this." He chuckles before shooting a naked one to the back of his throat. "Ahh," he sighs contentedly after it goes down.

"Wow. Okay, next." I shoot back the one from Maine. "See, it's milder. I don't like it as much."

He eats his, and his eyes look hungry, but not for food. He's looking at me intently, and as much as it excites me, I'm nervous. We're flirting and dancing around the elephant in the room. By that, I mean, how are we going to work together and not end up together-together?

"I like them both," he comments as we both reach for the last one.

"Canadian. These are my favorite as they have that tiny bite to them."

He clears his palate with a sip of wine, then eats the last oyster. After a moment, he pronounces his verdict.

"You're right. Canadian oysters are the best."

"I told you," I tease. I'm feeling the warmth of the wine that is making my body relax. There is also a warmth between my legs… well. Let's just say that oysters can sometimes do that to me, but today, I know it's the hot number on the other side of the table. I wonder how much longer I can contain myself.

Emily, shake it off, I tell myself. This could jeopardize both our careers. It's not illegal, but definitely unprofessional and frowned upon to have an affair with my client.

And if I'm representing him legally, like reading over any contracts, an even dumber move. If we had a physical relationship and it interfered with me representing him, then I'd have to step away from his case. Do I want him as a client or a lover? And if he's my lover, would it be worth it? How long could it last, realistically?

"So tonight we have the game, and tomorrow we're meeting with the team's promoters to talk about a fundraiser," Wyatt recaps as he drains the wine from his glass.

"Yep." I sit taller in my seat and lean on the table. "It will be a fun event. I might be able to meet some more hockey players," I tease, finding it impossible to stop flirting even though I know it's wrong. "Hmm, I wonder what players would be willing to take to the ice and help kids play hockey?"

"What players wouldn't? To us, this is our life. It's important for us to pass the love of the game on to others."

"You have a point," I nod in agreement as the oyster plate of ice and shells is removed and our lunch is served.

"Well, dig in because it's overpriced burgers and fries at the rink tonight," I tease.

"And that's just the first course." He gives me another devilish grin that I am becoming accustomed to.

Oh, boy.

By the end of lunch, we decide that we like this place and designate it as 'our place.' Seeing the city for the first time together, all these memories will be etched in our minds for a long time, whether anything physical happens between us or not.

I MIGHT BE GETTING USED to the cold weather because my nipples aren't completely frozen as we step back into Wyatt's condo. I immediately take the puppy out, and when I return, I'm hit with a carb overload. In the middle of playing with Mika, the tiredness overcomes me, and I fall asleep on the couch.

I vaguely remember a blanket being laid over me as I drifted off, but I might have imagined it.

When I wake up, I check my watch, and it's two hours later.

"Morning sunshine," Wyatt teases, his face is close to mine. "Well, more like afternoon. We have to head to the arena. I have to be there two hours before game time."

I sit up and hope I didn't drool on the couch. Oh no, what if my makeup rubbed off on his white couch? Dare I look?

I surreptitiously glance at the couch as I get up, and by some miracle, it's still not messed up, though I'm sure it's only a matter of time with Mika around.

"I need to feed the little one." I yawn as I finally stand.

"Already did, and walked her too. She's getting used to the leash, although she'd rather carry it in her mouth."

"Aww, that's so cute. It shows she still wants to be independent – like she's walking herself by holding the leash in her mouth. And it's kinda of like a pacifier, too. How soon do we need to take her to the vet?"

"Not we, you. Your dog," he reminds me.

"I didn't mean anything by it–" I start apologizing, but he interrupts me by saying he's just busting my balls.

"Seriously, though, the sooner, the better; she probably needs shots and who knows what else."

"Right, well, I'll call one tomorrow."

"Great." He disappears into his room, then returns with a team practice jersey, and hands it to me.

"This is so cool. For real? I can wear it?"

"I figure one of us should have our team's jersey on for the game," he says dully as he shrugs his shoulders.

"Good point."

I can tell he's bummed about not playing as we make our way to the arena for tonight's game, and I can't blame him. In fact, it makes me more committed to righting this wrong and making sure my fundraising and PR event goes off perfectly.

15

———

WYATT

It feels strange driving to the arena knowing I won't be playing tonight. I don't understand why the management here can't be more graceful and forgiving. But I guess even if I did nothing wrong, I let my team down.

"I hear that the girlfriends and wives of hockey players, well, all sports I imagine, have a serious class system and pecking order," Emily says, interrupting my train of thought. I'm glad to get out of my head and into a conversation with her.

"They do. It's not as bad at the lower divisions because no one is a big success yet, but there are still some drama mamas here and there. The pros are tough and not just on us players. Management doesn't like drama that reaches the locker room or our players' heads."

"Not to mention unwelcome media attention and scrutiny. That's why you're benched."

"Yep, though I can't believe the media ever cared about what happened." I turn a blinker on and turn onto a road I travel at least every other day.

Between team practice, extra workouts, and getting together with my trainer, it's a full-time job. I mean, it's not like we work for eight hours straight. The hours are all over the place, but they add up. And traveling sucks up a lot of time.

"Here we are. This is the parking lot reserved for players," I point to the back of the Camden Bay Arena. We circle around the monolithic sports complex.

"Wow, is this all you guys drive in winter? Huge SUVs? I was expecting rows of sports cars!" Emily's lack of enthusiasm makes me wish I had my Mustang.

"Yeah, good luck with that in winter, Florida girl. Nice sports cars should not be on the road after the first fresh powder. They all go into storage because of the salt on the roads. Can't drive a Mustang with your feet sticking out the rusted bottom like Barney Rubble."

"Damn, I was hoping I'd get a ride in a Ferrari or Lamborghini!"

I'm surprised she's a car fanatic and look over to see if she's putting me on. Instead, she flashes me a smile even though I know she's disappointed. Her trench coat is open just enough for me to decide she looks good in purple, blue, and white.

"You look great. My team colors...you wear them well."

"Thanks!"

"Your boots, on the other hand…" I trail off and shake my head.

"Oh you," she takes a swing at my shoulder and barely taps it with her fingers. "Fine, I'm going shopping tomorrow. What footwear should I get?"

"Okay, I know it might look a bit rugged for your taste, but get something with Gore-Tex in it, so you don't get wet feet for starters. I'm surprised those are still glued together, to be honest."

I might sound like I'm lecturing her but seriously, she needs better cold-weather clothing, "It will also keep you from slipping, although you're still more than welcome to hang onto my arm, just in case." I smile and puff my chest out.

From the way her sweater dress underneath the team jersey hugs her hips, I can tell they are rounded and full, like her breasts. Damn this cold weather and girls having to cover up all their fun parts.

There's nothing better about summertime than seeing pert, hard nipples through a bikini top or a white t-shirt. I doubt Emily would be impressed with where my mind wanders. Sorry, Emily. I'm a dude.

I adjust myself in the seat and try to push down my erection. She looks even sexier in my jersey. I can only imagine what her legs must look like without her leggings. All I can see are delicate ankles and long slender legs.

"You've been to a game before, right?"

"Sure, the team in Fort Myers, the Gators, but other than that, I don't have a bucket list to see every arena or team in the country. You're still in the hunt for the playoffs, right?"

"Well, sort of. Right now we're barely hanging onto the wild card slot, so we need to up our game. It's always better to have our seat at the table rather than to have to rely on the dreaded Wild Card."

"Seat at the table," she snickers. "Godfather references? In hockey?"

"Who doesn't like The Godfather?"

"I find it confusing, but I know everyone says it was one of the better films of the 70s."

"Maybe it's more of a guy movie," I admit while driving around looking for a spot.

"And why is it bad finishing as a wild card? As long as you guys make it to the finals, you're still in it."

"Hum—well, it's kind of…you're treated like a case of warts when you're a wild card. All the other team's fans diss you for unseating their higher-ranked guys in the race to the Cup. You know?"

"I get it, I've heard that before. So, can you guys do better, or is there a problem?"

"Some problems are easier to spot than others. I haven't been with the team long enough to know the team dynamics, like how healthy our star players are, that sort of stuff."

"That's fine, I don't need to know any secrets. Wow, it gets dark so early up here," she says, changing the subject as she looks out her passenger window.

"Funny, 'up here.'"

"Well, it is! I never really thought about how much farther north you are. Right now, it would still be light back home."

"Yeah, the sun comes around quickly as well. There is a place in Maine that is the first continental land in the United States to see the sun every morning. Sometimes it's Washington County, others, it's Mount Katahdin."

"Really? Did you read that on a tourist brochure?" She looks at me in amazement.

"Haha, no. I should have mentioned it to you earlier, I have a knack for retaining useless information. It's my superpower."

"Well, in any case, you sound just like the brochures I read at my hotel when I'm looking for some stuff to do now that I might be here a while."

Wait a minute. Did she say she'll be here a while?

I try to make it sound casual. "What's that about staying here longer?"

I park in a spot and help Emily make it safely to the team's entrance while she fills me in.

"Well, when I took this assignment, I thought it would be a quick in-and-out trip, but I should know by now that the powers that be don't work that fast. We have our meeting tomorrow, but a fundraiser could take a month to organize, and even then that's pretty rushed," she explains.

"Well, you're the expert." I hand her off to the equipment manager to show her to our seats.

"Here's a ticket, just in case," I say, handing a printed ticket to Emily. "I'll be up before the game starts."

"Okay," she replies, turning to follow the equipment manager.

Did I hear a touch of disappointment in her voice?

The guys are all bustling around me. I barely hear the music booming out of Luc's Bluetooth speaker. I watch Emily walk away, and I'm not ashamed to admit that it's a great opportunity to enjoy the view of her hips swaying.

Now it's game time. I want to be a good sport about things, so I put on a smile even though I don't feel happy about being benched. Fake it till you make it, right?

"Alexandre!" We bump fists and do the "kaboom" thing, opening our fists after pulling it back from the tap.

"Wyatt! How are ya' man? Knocked up that agent of yours yet?" he teases me.

"We'll see if the first round takes," I quip, realizing it's probably too soon after the Sylvia thing to be making jokes like that. Thankfully the music was loud, and Luc didn't hear me.

My entire life, I thought making it to the pros was going to be based on my skill set, being the best at what I do, and nothing else. Now, I realize all this other political stuff must be confined to the locker room, or it can end our careers.

"So, we're going to do a fundraiser skate, I think," I volunteer to Alexandre as he rubs some salve into his right shoulder before pulling his chest protector on.

"That's cool. You'll need the most popular faces on the team." His matter-of-fact tone makes it seem like it's no big deal.

Maybe it isn't. Maybe I worry too much.

"Hmm, let's see, I'd say Victor Karlsson and Sean Ian. Those guys are the top two when it comes to selling the most jerseys and their faces are plastered on every billboard in town. Well, goalies are always popular as well, but you've seen McDavid," he says, trying not to laugh and almost spitting out the sports drink he tipped in his mouth not five seconds ago.

Alexandre gets his fluids under control. "Trust me, it will be fine," he pauses as he pulls equipment out of his locker. "Just don't go near the coach's daughter."

"Coach has a daughter? I thought she was, like, ten."

He raises a finger. "Ah, see, there's where what you don't know bites ya' in the ass. His smoking hot daughter was college as far as I know."

"Fuck, I didn't know that."

"I know you didn't, eh? Relax, I got ya' man." He laughs and taps my shoulder with his hand before putting on more gear.

The room is abuzz with one-liners and banter. If we aren't ready for the game now, we'll never be. We've done all our homework and we even got the low down on the other team's weak points. Our strategy is to run the Buffalo Blazers up and down the boards to tire them out. They aren't good with the dump and chase, so we will use it against them.

"We." I guess today I should be thinking of it as "they." Damn. I love hockey. It's fluid, it's fast, and things are constantly changing. Well, maybe things will change in my favor and it'll be "we" again soon. It's going to be brutal watching from the stands.

I exchange some banter with Alexandre and make sure to say hi to Victor and Sean, so they know my face, seeing as how I'll probably be seeing them again soon. Last but not least, I approach Luc and tell him to have a good game before making my exit. He doesn't look like he wants to take my head off so, all in all, I think things are looking up.

16

EMILY

Wyatt is so handsome. Sometimes, I need someone to pinch me, he's that gorgeous. I take note of his strong jawline and perfect profile as we pass under the streetlights on our way to the rink. He might be young, but he's smart, and I like how he reads human behavior so well for a man his age. Astute, that's it. He is definitely older than his years.

I find my seat on the lower level of the arena and enjoy the low murmur of the crowd as people trickle in carrying food, beer, and kids. The house lights are all on and I'm at a loss as to what to do besides play on my phone. Since I don't know how long Wyatt will be, I text Natalie. She should be home by now even with a horrendous rush hour.

She responds immediately.

Hey girl, what's up? Busy with that golf event, wish you were here. I have to man the registration table. Ugg. I'll have to work all weekend to boot.

Sorry about that, but it's a good cause. Besides, it's a day in the sunshine while I'm freezing my ass off. Dan is doing good, by the way.

I heard, I'm glad, he's nice. How is your mission going?

Going. He's so freaking cute. I don't know what to do. I left my vibrator at home. But oh, my. These players are hot.

Girl, jump on that.

I can't. I'm here to fix what happened the last time he jumped on something!

That doesn't seem fair.

Life rarely is.

And then I think to myself that I've been ripped off. If we had met under normal circumstances, things could have transpired naturally. As it stands, we're both screwed and not in a good way. I mean, he winked at me, that has to mean something. Doesn't it?

Have I been away from dating so long I've forgotten the standard universal social cues of crushing on someone? Maybe Natalie needs to give me the current 411 on flirting. I know to flip my hair and bat my eyelashes, but maybe there's something new.

I mean, if Wyatt is turned on by thermal underwear and three layers of socks with the proper footwear …now you're talking. Maybe to him, that is sexy. Goodness knows the winters last for six months here. And I heard even during summer months, the temperatures only reach the low 70s.

Come on. If I lived here, my pubes would turn into permafrost.

Natalie, I can't be the cause of him getting an even worse reputation and possibly being traded down to the minors or another team.

To have that happen without it having anything to do with his performance on the ice, is just wrong.

I see what you mean, but sometimes, things have a way of working out. Do you have a plan?

Yeah, a PR event that raises money for the GM's favorite charity should work well. I'll iron out the details tomorrow.

I hear the door to the ice rink slam and a ref skates around the ice.

The game's starting, TTYL.

See ya, keep me posted.

I slip my phone into my purse and turn to see Wyatt take the steps three at a time to come up from the bottom floor. He drops into the seat next to me, looking pretty happy, all things considered.

"How did the meet and greet with the guys go?"

"Great. I even wished the goalie luck, and he wasn't a jerk so that's an improvement."

"Sounds like it."

The stands are filling up, and I smell the cinnamon-roasted pecans wafting over me from someone in the section behind us.

"Those pecans smell delicious, but I'm still stuffed from lunch."

"I thought you were doing burgers and fries."

"Nah, I'm fine, maybe just a soda."

"I'll get it." He jumps up, asks me what kind, and disappears.

He returns a few minutes later with my drink.

"Thanks, wow, that was quick."

"Connections."

Why do I have the feeling his connections involve his grin or a wink?

He pulls a Mauler's cap out of his back pocket and puts it on his head.

I lean back to take him in.

"Fans, cameras," he explains.

"Oh, yeah, forgot about that. I rarely see you guys sitting back here on National TV."

"Good, let's try to keep it that way," he says grimly.

No kidding.

The arena gets noisier as it fills with fans, and we both like to people-watch. We are commenting on the cute babies we see, there are kids carrying signs as big as them, and then there are the most spirited couples.

We sit, talk, and chuckle like we've known each other since first grade.

But we haven't. It's only our second day together. I take that as a sign. I've never felt this comfortable with someone on a first or is that a third date?

We might get away with an affair but not in public. Fans pile in next to us, and I give him a sly look, and we both laugh. It's like we're getting away with something, and yet nothing at the same time.

But we're in on the joke together. That's what matters.

The Zamboni cruises around the ice, the Mauler's pep squad skates around afterward, scooping up some ice that looks like snow cone shavings, and the nets are put up.

Half the arena is covered in a sea of purple and white, and seeing as there are always fans from the opponent's team, there are quite a few blue and black jerseys in the stands as well.

"I wonder how many fans come here from New York."

"No telling. But it's gotta be cheaper than seeing the team play in New York, even with the travel."

"Good point."

"It's pretty nice in Maine. I mean, if you like snow. This rink is nice. You have at least one good Italian restaurant we know of. I'd say it's looking better than my first day here."

"Ha, you were not a happy camper at the lake!"

"No, I wasn't…but in my defense, I was hungry. My flight was delayed due to the weather. I'm used to getting on a flight and arriving home on time, like normal."

"Oh, God, the longer you travel, the more you realize you're lucky if it all goes as planned. Tornados, El Niño storms, and tons of weird stuff happen. I know these things."

"I see." I cock my head to the side, watching the pep squad work for the crowd as the music has started. "Well, it wasn't on the hotel brochure," I say and a chuckle escapes my lips. Lips that wouldn't mind feeling bruised because I was kissed too hard.

"Any minute now," he remarks, pulling at the cuff of his dress shirt to reveal a gold-plated analog watch. So much for my thoughts of a hot kiss.

"Wow, a real watch."

"Yeah, kind of a throwback to simpler times. I learned how to tell time on my dad's watch."

"Aww, I did too. And then I had a Mickey Mouse watch. Sad that kids don't wear them much anymore."

I take a long drag on my straw. If I keep drinking the soda this fast, I'm going to spend the entire night peeing.

The players come out for their two-minute warm-up and Wyatt leans forward, placing his elbows on his knees. He's watching his teammates like a perched Mama eagle watches her eaglets.

After the warmup, the music stops. "At this time, please stand," comes over the speakers.

"Looks like McDavid is ready," Wyatt comments as we stand for the national anthem. Then they move on to honoring Veterans and charities who've received donations from the team's fundraising.

I take the opportunity to visit the ladies' room and hope I remember the way back to my seat. I'm known to be terrible with directions, but I have my purse and Wyatt has his phone.

Sure enough, I get confused returning and have to pop in a few entrances to the lower section before I spot Wyatt in his ball cap. As I make my way back to my seat, I think about it again. He makes having a boyfriend look like an enticing proposition.

Ultimately, the game is a blast with me yelling like a wild woman and Wyatt doesn't seem to mind. In fact, I think he likes how into the game I am. We have a resounding win at 5-2, and if the team below us loses tomorrow, we'll move up in the standings. I hope Wyatt's penance is served, and he'll be back on the ice for the next game. This playoff race thing is exciting!

The evening is a crash course on everything I didn't know I needed to know about hockey. I enjoy it. It's been so long since I was out on a 'date,' well, not a date but, y'know, grown-up time. And for once, it's after seven-thirty, and I'm not home for the night.

I'm beginning to have fun, and I want more.

We leave the arena, picking up some burgers and fries from a drive-thru as we're both starving.

"Oh, we have to get back to Mika. I bet she's made a mess. We've been gone so long. I probably should have bought a kennel."

"Good idea, and you can use it to take her home or maybe a carrying case."

"I'll look tomorrow."

We go upstairs, and once inside, Mika runs to us so fast she slides on the floor and crashes into my hands as I attempt to help her stop.

"Crazy girl, crashing into the Emily boards like that," Wyatt jokes as he pets her head and removes his coat.

I crack up at his hockey reference, and as I rise, our bodies are inches apart. I smell the clean scent of his cologne.

"I'll just take her out." I'm reaching for her leash that's behind him on the wall.

"Umm…I'll clean the floor." And there went our opportunity for a real kiss.

When I return, Wyatt has changed into track pants and a t-shirt.

"It's late, I need to get going. Can I pick you up tomorrow? Nine-thirty, sharp?"

"Sure, thanks." He hangs off his heavy condo door as Mika plays with the shoelaces in his trendy sneakers. God, I hope those shoes don't get chewed to death.

"I had a great time tonight."

"Me too," he says, and his face is so close to mine that I feel the hair on the back of my neck rise.

"I'll see you tomorrow." He slowly closes the door. Mika stays inside, and I'm left staring at them. I'm a little hurt and more than a little confused.

I wonder if he's playing hard to get or if the recent Sylvia events have put him off women.

Maybe I need to sex myself up. It's day two, and we spend as much time together as we are apart.

I contemplate this on my way to my quiet, bleak room.

It's for the best.

Wyatt did the right thing, whether he wanted to kiss me or not.

Damn.

17

WYATT

I'm doing the right thing, sleeping with a puppy, not Emily, but it's killing me.

I remind myself that being a good boy will hopefully rectify the bad opinion that the GM and William Barber currently have of me, both savvy businessmen who are too keen to believe rumors rather than listen to the new kid–someone they don't know and have never met.

As Alexandre pointed out, don't get involved with someone you meet in a bar after knowing them for just two minutes. That is solid advice in retrospect. But the thought of the right woman, a mature, gorgeous woman like Emily, to keep me warm at night is what I cling to when I need to convince myself the world isn't all bad.

I take Mika outside one more time before shucking my clothes and crawling into bed with only thoughts of Emily to warm my cold sheets. I'm anxious about tomorrow, and I can't fall asleep.

It sucked being a healthy scratch, but at least watching the game with Emily made it less depressing. I wish she could see me play, really play.

Maybe I'm deluding myself. It's presumptuous of me to think she would be open to dating me. But I've noticed her stealing glances at me and playing with her hair the way girls do when they're interested.

She hasn't made a move but might be trying to keep it professional. I've never been in this situation before. I'm unsure what my next move should be. But she's not going to be here forever, so the clock is ticking. I have to make a move before it's too late.

I know, I know. After the last fiasco, I swore off women and dating, and here I am caving in less than a week. But we get along so well, and she's hot as blazes. Crap.

Mika snuggles behind my legs and keeps me warm as I drift to sleep. The last thing I remember is the smell of vanilla sugar cookies, a scent that reminds me of Emily.

EMILY CALLS me from the car on her way over to ask if I'll take Mika out since she's dressed up and wearing heels. I'm wearing my best suit, a suit I was told to get months ago. I spent more than I wanted to at the time, but now I'm thankful I did. I need to get more suits like this, but I've decided to hold off for now. I'm new, and I've hit a snag without anticipating it. I'd rather not jinx things any further.

Watching Mika play in the snow, I'm not sure taking her to Florida is a great idea. All her fur is great now, but the summer sun in the south is another matter. Picking her up, she feels like she's put on a few pounds since she's been with me. I think she's happy here.

I deposited Mika back in my condo before returning to the lobby. My heart is pounding in my chest as Emily pulls up. I try to relax my shoulders, but I'm anxious for the day to start. It's a big one for both of us.

"Hi, how are you?" I ask, opening the passenger door.

"Great, thanks for taking care of Mika."

"No problem. Are you ready?" I ask, folding myself into her car.

"Oh, yeah, piece of cake, I'm used to large meetings."

"Great," I reply, noticing Emily waits until my seatbelt clicks into place before moving the car forward.

"If I'm not going the right way, let me know."

"Will do," I answer. I stare out the window to distract myself from how hot she looks in a business suit.

After a small talk in the car, we walk briskly from the parking lot to the arena. I lead Emily to the main offices on the second floor. Her heels click on the tiled floor, and I stay close in case she should stumble.

She's wearing a dark blue pinstriped suit with a pencil skirt that shows off her curvy hips and falls modestly just above her knees. The mint green silk shirt under her blazer changes the color of her eyes to blue-green. I could happily stare into those eyes all day.

The doors to the boardroom are open, ready for our arrival. I first notice a table full of coffee, tea, and, as Emily says, carb-loaded breakfast pastries.

We pick our seats at the table, Emily reserving her spot with her briefcase and purse before we head to the refreshments table. At this hour, who doesn't want more coffee?

With a mug of coffee in her left hand, Emily casually and expertly works the room, introducing herself and me when needed. Her confidence rubs off on me. I begin to relax. I'm not comfortable around suits yet. But I can make being six feet tall and weighing 190 pounds look good.

"The GM is in Florida for the golf tournament. Natalie confirmed that when she texted me this morning. With him out of the way, it will be easier to work with his staff, or so I think. Less pressure," she whispers to me.

"Oh," is all I can come up with. I feel like a lone minnow surrounded by a school of betta fish, but I stand tall with my chin up, shoulders back, and feet squarely set apart. A guy my size cannot hide, so I might as well use it to my advantage and make my presence known.

Emily approaches a man in his forties with salt and pepper hair who appears to be in charge. She asks him if he'd like to begin.

Mr. Devonshire is the head of the public relations team employed by the team, and as he puts it, "We're due for a fundraiser, so let's see what you have." He gives us a weak smile, and I get the impression that's his best effort on any given day.

Emily takes over. "I propose an event with Wyatt and your top four players to skate with kids as a fundraiser. Afterward, we can use the company's club dining area for appetizers and drinks. The players will mingle with the guests, and the press will be invited, naturally."

She passes around a packet of information to everyone.

"I propose we start the event at ten in the morning and conclude at one. Dan, the owner of Sports and Entertainment Enterprises will provide the food. We'll line up tables for the sponsors and live music in the downstairs atrium near the lobby."

"There will be games for the kids around the arena walkways, which will be advertised as a family day. There is a fee for the kids to join the open skate with the players and obtain signatures. I propose we send invites to boosters with all the proceeds going to the General Manager's favorite charity. With all the youth hockey teams and outdoor skating rinks in the area. I think it's a great match."

The eight men and women at the table are flipping through the packets in front of them, and judging from their reaction, I think her presentation is going well. Damn, she's good at this.

"I believe there are some backpacks left over from the back-to-school drive earlier this year and some t-shirts. We can offer a give-away to each registrant. The number allowed to register will be strictly limited to create a sense of exclusivity. I'd love to call it the Great Celebrity Skate, but whatever you think will go over best is fine. You know your audience better than I do." She smiles and looks around the room.

Mr. Devonshire is impressed. "Wow, you came prepared. You've left so little for us to do."

"I think I'll only need help with the live band and securing a big-screen TV to show video clips in the VIP area reserved for the large donors, where we'll serve them appetizers and drinks. The other guests can eat at limited stations opened just for them. That way the arena won't be filled, and the event's intimacy is protected. That should motivate families to bring kids in, especially in the middle of the coldest month here."

Mr. Devonshire looks up from the proposal and says, "We'll have our legal team look it over. As you probably know, Dan and Gary are pretty good friends. I think it's a great idea. I don't think Gary will have an issue with it."

"Great, I heard your General Manager and Dan are friends. I find it ironic that he's in Florida, where I should be, and I'm here, where he should be." She lets out a small laugh, and the room comes alive as all the tension dissipates with her smile.

And her smile can do that. She doesn't even know she has that much power over people.

The group loosens up and starts telling jokes about the Florida humidity, and before I know it, we're standing and shaking hands. The only details left to be ironed out are the date for the event, what band to hire, and to start making phone calls to get the deposits and staffing organized.

The arena has enough staff to handle it, but I'm sure Emily will stay on top of everything and make sure it's done the way she wishes and to her standards.

We leave, and I commend her on how skillfully she can work a room.

She elbows me slightly as she turns to me and grins. "Why do you think Dan likes me to go to these things with him?"

"Well, I've witnessed firsthand what an asset you are, and I have to say, I'm impressed. Do you think I'll be back on the team now? We have a road trip starting tomorrow."

"We'll see. I'll put a call into Dan."

I like this putting-a-call-in-to-Dan idea. He seems to be the go-to guy. I look forward to meeting him in person soon instead of just over phone calls and videos.

WE GRAB A LATE AFTERNOON LUNCH, and by the time we get back to my place, Emily can't wait to flick her heels off and collapse onto the couch. When I return from taking Mika out, I flop on the couch beside her.

My phone dings. I check my messages.

I jump up, pumping my arm and fist in the air, exclaiming, "Yes!"

"What?" Emily bolts upright as the pup pees on the floor, unsure of what is happening.

"That was Coach. I'm back on the game roster tomorrow, so I'll fly out in the morning. We're playing Buffalo. They were here. Now we go there."

I quickly text Alexandre the good news, then pull Emily up and give her a huge bear hug. She squeals like a teenage girl before letting out a hearty laugh as I spin her around.

Dizzy, she collapses into my strong arms, and my cock joins the celebration. Her smoking-hot body is in my arms. I look deep into her eyes, and my vows of celibacy evaporate. Like a bear coming out of hibernation and hungry for nourishment, my lips claim hers savagely. Our kiss lasts so long that my lungs scream for air. Me, a hockey player, needs to surface for air. Don't tell my trainer.

After coming up for air, we continued. My kisses were relentless, nipping on her lower lip. She kisses me hard in return, wrapping her arms around my neck and pulling me closer. I scoop her up while dropping kisses and sucking on her neck. I steer her towards my bedroom.

I sit her gently on the bed and chuck off my shoes and clothes as quickly as possible while she fumbles with the tiny buttons of her silk shirt.

"Are you sure this is okay? This isn't a conflict of interest?" she murmurs as I drop my boxers, and my hard cock springs out.

"Not on my end, it's not," I pant as I slip off her shirt and skillfully unclasp her black lacy bra.

For a woman on a business trip, she dresses sexy underneath the tough veneer of the power suit.

18

EMILY

I hope he doesn't change his mind and stop because there is no way I want out of this. Definitely...not.

"I'll be out of town tomorrow," he murmurs as he runs his tongue up my neck. I feel goosebumps, but not because I'm cold. "You'll have to stay here to watch Mika."

"Umm…" All I can think about is the fact that I have the man of my dreams beside me. When he runs his slender fingers down the side of my naked body, my abs involuntarily flinch.

"Does that tickle?"

"No, I just didn't expect it to feel like…that."

"Like what?"

"Your touch makes me warm and…I'm very, very, wet," I tell him as I run my hands over his hard as fuck round ass. I wasn't sure exactly how round until now. But yes, he has the perfect bubble butt.

I particularly love to grab them, so I dig my nails in, and his grin tells me this makes him happy. He responds by reaching between my legs, and his fingers enter me.

"Oh," I gasped, arching my back to give him more access.

"Does that feel good?"

"Oh, yeah…" My voice fades as pleasure ripples up my body.

He pulls his fingers out and puts them in my mouth so I can taste myself as his eyes meet mine.

This is really happening.

I run my hands down his back and up his sinewy abs.

"Hmm," he moans as he drops kisses on my abdomen and moves further down my body. He explores my wetness with the tip of his tongue, and I feel like I'm floating.

I run my hands through his hair, tugging harder as the pressure builds within me.

He hovers over me and slowly slides his thick cock inside me, filling every inch of me as we hungrily devour each other in a deep kiss.

Supporting himself on his arms, he moves back and forth inside me, while I look deep into his brown eyes, getting lost in their intensity.

He's looking into mine, too; eyes which used to be so cold and judgmental of jocks. It comes with the territory. I can't help buying into the stigma attached to guys who know they are the standard by which so many other young men measure themselves.

Getting to know Wyatt makes them more human to me. Now, I see him as a man, one who is fun and not afraid to love again, even if he says he's sworn off women. The fact his cock is inside me right now—I have no clue what it means, other than lust.

Normally, I'd like to have some indication a hookup will lead to more. But in this case, I have to let go of the steering wheel, so to speak, and see where this goes. I need to enjoy the moment and not dwell on the fact I'm older and this is crazy.

His lips claim mine and I burn this moment into my memory because if this is just a one-week fling, I want to remember it forever.

Bending his head to one breast, he places his warm lips on my nipple. He suckles and nibbles making it even harder and causing muscles deep within my abdomen to tighten.

His hand grabs my other breast, and his soft, supple fingers squeeze my tight little peak. He rubs it between his fingertips, faster, then slower, breaking up the pace and throwing my rising orgasm off course.

I thought I'd come more quickly than this but prolonging it has its benefits. I reach up to his face and feel the beginning of rough hair sprouting along his jawline and trace my finger down a scar on his chin as I look deep into his eyes, unafraid to meet his intensity for the first time.

"Am I too rough?" His deep bedroom voice turns me on and so does his consideration as to how I feel.

"Not at all." I slide my fingers behind his neck pulling his lips towards mine.

His rhythm picks up as his hands move to my butt, pulling me closer to him. We lock lips as his long strokes smooth out and become faster and faster. The excitement and desire reach their apex, and I can't hold back anymore.

"Ahh." I break free, wanting to stay with him and yet I'm detached, soaring.

He pounds me harder and faster, sending me over the edge, and I'm in another world where I'm floating and falling at the same time.

"Uhh," he cries out and his body shudders as he comes. He stays inside me, his dick pulsing and still hard, dropping little kisses on my shoulder and a longer, lingering one on my lips until finally, he slumps on top of me, exhausted.

"Wow," I murmur, running my fingers through his thick hair.

"Yeah." His breathing is jagged and labored.

"That was incredible."

He rolls onto his back. "Yes, it was."

Rolling onto my side, I place a hand on his chest and watch it rise and fall with his heavy breathing.

"Wow. I missed one game and look at me. I'm all out of shape," he jokes, taking a minute to regain his breathing.

"So, you have an away game tomorrow?" I ask while smoothing his chest hair with my fingers.

"Yeah, I do. I'll leave you a key so you can take care of Mika. I leave in the morning but make yourself at home." He picks up my hand and kisses it.

"You sure?"

"Of course, unless you want to give her up for adoption."

"No way," I protest as I slap his chest lightly. "I can't possibly give her up."

"Relax, I'm teasing. I know how much you love the little fur ball."

"I know. Even though I've heard some people call them German Shedders. I mean, it's cold now, and she's not shedding much but can you imagine her in Florida's heat?"

"Ha, good luck with that," is all he can say.

"And I'm not sure how she'll do in a condo. A dog this size should have a big yard."

"True, but it will work out. I'm sure it will."

"I could live cheaper if I give up my condo. I just didn't want a house because my maintenance skills are limited to changing light bulbs and air conditioning filters."

"I'm sure you can do more, just Google it or find a YouTube video."

"You have such faith in me," I reply.

We're quiet for a bit. I can't tell if today's hook-up is a one-time thing or not. There's no rule book on what the proper protocol is. "Maybe I should be going?"

"Stay, it's late afternoon. What do you have to rush off for?"

"You sure?"

"Very sure. Do you want anything?"

I feel a draft as he's no longer covering my body. "Maybe a blanket," I say, and get up to retrieve the comforter at the end of the bed.

"Nice view," he chuckles, slapping my ass which takes me by surprise.

"Oh, really?" I quip.

"Yep. I love your ass." He fluffs up a pillow and rests his head on it.

"Well, yours is pretty cute too."

"Come here." He coaxes me back into his arms, and I go willingly.

I lay my head on his chest and listened to his heartbeat.

After a comfortable silence, I ask, "What time do you fly out?"

"We meet at nine."

"Can I drop you off?" I ask, aware of how my professional life is overlapping my personal one for the first time.

"I'll drive. We'd better be careful in public."

"Right, oh boy, an occupational hazard already." I raise my head and look him squarely in the eye. "Look, I've never done this before. I don't want you to get the impression I make it a habit of sleeping with my clients."

"I know you wouldn't. I've had more than my share of women, but it never meant much to me, and always left me feeling empty and lonely afterwards."

"I know that feeling," I agree. Maybe it's why I've avoided dating for so long.

"But you're different," he says.

"It's the dog, isn't it?" I deadpan in an attempt to lighten the mood.

"Maybe," he grins, "but I've been a terrible host. We need to go out so I can show you the town."

"Like what?'

"Why don't you leave that to me? When I get back, plan to spend the day with me."

"Okay." Maybe this isn't one of those one-off things, after all.

"So why don't we take this little puppy for a walk and a trip to the vet? I made an appointment for her."

"You did?" This blows my mind. He's so thoughtful. It's not even his dog. I should have done it sooner myself. "Thanks, sorry, this puppy seems to be relying on you more than me," I sit up and pull the blanket around me.

"So, stay."

"What?"

"Stay here."

He pulls my mouth to his and gives me a long kiss, his tongue entwined with mine. I think we might be going for round two, but he pulls back and asks if I'm hungry.

"I'd love to," I whisper against his mouth.

He has no idea how hungry he makes me. And how well he fills in all the emptiness loneliness brings and no one sees.

MIKA IS A WELL-BEHAVED superstar at her vet appointment, and we drop her off at home before heading to the local grocery store to pick up steaks and sides to go with it. I pick out a not-so-cheap red wine, fully intending to cover it, but he won't let me pay for anything.

"Seriously, Wyatt, you paid for the vet. Let me pay for the food." I might as well have been shouting into an abandoned cave for all the good it did me.

"Nope. No way." He bats my hand aside and slides his platinum credit card into the machine.

I load bags full of food into the cart.

He pushes it, loads up the trunk, and opens the door for me.

I don't want to be a smartass and ask if he always does this or if he's trying to impress me. I guess time will tell.

But I'm not a patient person, especially when it comes to a man I'm interested in. For now, I will enjoy the attention.

We have a good time cooking together. He wraps potatoes in foil, and I coat them with butter and seasoning and toss them straight onto the rack in the oven.

When I realize he's going to cook the steaks indoors on a gas stove with a built-in grill plate, I hold my breath it won't set off the smoke alarm. While he's letting the grill heat up, I make what I intended to be a small tossed salad, but it ends up being enough for six people.

"Damn, are you half rabbit?" he quips.

I giggle. "I love salads, all the different flavors and textures." I mix the lettuce with shredded carrots, cut tomatoes, and cucumbers before adding croutons to the top.

He comes up behind me, wraps his arms around my waist, and nuzzles my neck. Mika gets in on the action and rubs up against us both.

"I think she likes us."

"Undoubtedly," he agrees, returning his attention to the steaks as the aroma fills the air.

"You know, the condo doesn't seem so static now. I think I just needed to start living my life, but with you here, it feels like home, and the ankle biter is cute." He pulls the steaks off the grill and places them on our plates.

"Hmm, well, I think this might be a miracle puppy. I didn't realize how alone I was until she stumbled into my life." I'm careful to word this carefully because I'm not getting my hopes up when it comes to us.

The hard facts are: he's a jock, he's not my boyfriend, and he happens to be younger than me. The last thing I want to do, is compete with the line of desperate horny women who throw themselves at the guys on a nightly basis.

That's not me. I am who I am. And I plan to take advantage of his time away tomorrow and visit the mall.

When we come back from taking Mika out, I agree to watch a Mark Walberg movie with him, but halfway through I'm falling asleep on his shoulder.

"Come, let's go to bed," he lifts me up, and I slide my arms around his neck.

And the round two that was hinted at earlier arrives with all the tells of a man and a woman in love. We aren't fucking, it's more than just two people going at it. I feel the love in every word we exchange, every touch, every kiss.

It's going to be hard to walk away from this.

WYATT LEAVES FOR THE AIRPORT, and I swing by my hotel room to pick up a few necessities, putting them in a bag to take to Wyatt's. Then I head to the mall, wondering what the girls ten years younger are wearing nowadays and if I'll find anything I like.

Parking the car at the mall, I'm happy to see some of my favorite stores. One thing is for sure. I'm guaranteed to find some winter clothing. The stores in Florida have a very limited selection because it never gets cold.

In Florida, if you are shopping for clothes to wear on a ski trip or Alaska cruise, you need to look in one of the expensive anchor stores. Because unless you're traveling up north, there is no reason to own cold-weather clothes. The smaller stores don't even bother to stock them.

I'm excited about my purchases. I did manage to find some more sexy lingerie and some sportswear with lycra to insulate me from the cold wind, per Wyatt's suggestion. He also playfully suggested Vaseline, but there's no way in hell I'm putting petroleum jelly on my face, even if I'm outside watching him play pond hockey.

My grandmother still uses it as a night cream on her face and hands. She looks incredible for her age, so maybe there's something to it.

I drive to Wyatt's building, and once inside the lobby, I take a minute to organize all my shopping bags. Shit! The concierge, Mr. Mackey, is at his desk. Dammit, I have no choice but to walk past him. I need to let Mika out, and Wyatt's game will be on TV soon.

Shit, shit, shit!

He's probably taking notes on everyone's comings and goings. A hat and sunglasses will do me no good. He knows who I am and who I'm staying with. That's his job. But hey, Wyatt gave me a key. I have a right to be here.

I'm cordial and acknowledge him as I approach. My personal things are buried at the bottom of the shopping bags to avoid the prying eyes of nosy neighbors.

"Good shopping day?"

"Yes, thank you," I say without slowing down.

"I see the pup is getting big."

"She is. Does the building allow dogs? I'm assuming it does."

"Sure does, even so, there's not much folks can get away with around here." He rubs his fingers together, suggesting a bribe.

So, Mr. Mackey can be bought. Good to know. I shake my head as I step into the elevator.

I let Mika out of her new crate and take her downstairs to play in the snow. She enjoys the freedom to leap about as she chases anything moving under her feet.

Winter and I have reached an understanding: she won't give me frostbite, and I won't curse the day she was invented.

As soon as the game begins, I'm glued to Wyatt's big screen TV, wishing they had more close-ups of him.

I forgot to see what social media was saying earlier and grab my phone.

The comments started when he did warmups this morning with the team. Crap missed that.

All the comments are positive, though, so that's a good thing.

I smile and relax. Then I hear the announcer say, "When Hildebrand jumps the boards, he's gone with his foot on the gas." This sports commentator used to play in the NHL, which makes me wonder if Wyatt has thought about what he will do when he retires.

Then I chastise myself for thinking so far into the future. He's so young, he's probably still trying to figure out what he wants for breakfast, never mind a life after hockey.

19

WYATT

I texted Emily after the game, asking if she saw my assist. She replies right away. I know before she answers me. She ends the message with cute emojis and I find I'm sporting a goofy grin on my face because I'm infatuated with her.

I have to say, I can't complain about how I've been treated since I've been back on the roster. Alexandre said that everyone, at one point or another, has spent time on the GM or Coach's shit list.

I know Alexandre has a bit of an ego, and he's spent his fair share of time in the penalty box, so that makes me feel better.

The energy in the locker room is back to normal, and I enjoy the camaraderie. Everything in life is humming along exceptionally well, and I pray it continues.

After the game, we all eat copious amounts of food before loading up on the team's chartered jet to fly home.

I can't stop thinking about Emily. I'm not thinking about her only when I'm playing because that takes all my focus. When I video call her, I can tell she's in my bed, and my heart grows three sizes, like the Grinch who gave Christmas back to Whoville.

"So?"

"You played awesome. Hockey is my number one sport!"

She's wearing pajamas, but I wish she were naked. Is it too much to ask her to take her clothes off? What am I thinking? It will only get me horny, and she's not here to help me with that, so I scrap the idea.

"Everything went great. The team was great."

"No problems?"

"None, it was a great trip." It's getting late. I'll still have to wear my suit on the flight back, which kinda sucks, but the dress code is part of the protocol. Who knows. Maybe I'll be one of the guys who develops enough flair that he makes the tabloids and fashion pages.

"When will you be home?"

"Around one or two, I imagine. Don't feel you need to stay up, get your sleep." I can't help but get excited knowing that I'll be home in a few hours and won't be crawling into an empty bed. I have a sudden vision of what my life would be like with Emily, coming home to her and Mika from the airport after every road game, and…whoa, I like it.

"Thanks. Have a safe flight."

"Will do."

I hang up, not knowing what I'm supposed to say to her beyond that. Are we a fling? A relationship? I think I know what I want it to be.

I have planned an incredible day for us tomorrow, and I hope she enjoys it. My goal is to get Emily to like winter. If we can become a couple, she needs to learn how to embrace the cold weather.

WHEN I GET HOME, it's two in the morning, and I try not to wake Emily as I take the pup out, hang up my business suit, and crawl into bed. Emily snuggles up to me, mumbles something groggily, and returns to sleep. I like that the mattress is warm, and I love how affectionate she is, not at all the frigid bitch I pegged her for when I first laid eyes on her.

Mika is growing on me, and I don't resent getting up for her in the middle of the night. I thought I would, but I don't. The three of us do make a cute family.

Can Emily withstand my constant travel and the winter conditions? Would she be able to give up her life at the beach? What about her work? And more importantly, would she be happy with a younger man? Can I keep her interest, and will we grow as a couple in spite of our age difference? I'm pretty mature for my age, but you never know.

One week with Emily isn't enough to know the answers to any of those questions, so I need to tap into that maturity and play it cool. As they say, Rome wasn't built in a day. Getting a smart, sexy, successful woman to fall in love with me will take everything I have up my sleeve and more.

Wrapping my arm around her, I drift off to sleep, trying to ignore the doubts and fears whispering in my ear. When I wake up and see her face, I'll be fine.

I SMELL FRESHLY BREWED coffee and open one eye to see Emily bringing me a cup.

"Good morning. What time is it?"

"It's nine. I didn't want to wake you."

"How did you sleep?" I ask, sitting up and taking the warm cup from her.

"Better after you got home. I think I like having you around." She's sitting on the edge of the bed.

"I know the feeling. Speaking of that," I glance at my phone on the nightstand, "we need to go."

Dammit, I'm naked with a boner, but there's no time to pull her under the covers and fuck her brains out.

"Go? Go where?"

"It's a surprise. You said you like fast cars. My car is in storage, but I can show you a fun time on something else that goes fast. Pack an overnight bag. I have tomorrow off. I assume you can work from your phone and laptop?"

"Sure. I'm letting the people at the arena handle most of the details, and Natalie can help after the golf event. The fundraiser itself might not be until next month, but it looks like my job here is about done." Her voice trails off, and I can tell she's not ready to leave.

Maybe I do have a shot with her.

"Okay, pack everything you have to stay warm. We might have to stop and pick up some more stuff for you."

"What? You make it sound like I dress like a homeless person or a schoolgirl, I'm not sure which."

"Well, the sexy schoolgirl thing, I can get behind that," I say as I swat her ass and give her my devilish grin, making the scar on my chin surface more than usual.

"Oh, you!" She throws a pillow at my head, and I catch it. Hockey players have cat-like reflexes. She'll have to try harder if she wants to get the jump on me.

"What? Schoolgirl outfits are kind of sexy. Ask any guy," I protest, defending the male population.

"Okay, so I could use your help getting a warmer coat and… boots. I'm tired of wearing these practically every day since I got here. I have sneakers for today."

"Now you're talking!" I spring out of bed and open my duffle bag from yesterday, switching out a few items.

"I don't have anything that size," Emily says, looking at my small bag.

"No problem, I have more," I say, reaching into my closet and pulling out a duffle for her.

"Thanks, I'll text Natalie from the car just to let her know where I am today."

"Great. I'm free and clear," I say, closing my bag. Crap! I forgot about Mika, as I noticed her sleeping under my feet.

I texted Alexandre asking for a huge favor for just one night.

He reluctantly agrees, but I know he's already trying to think of something as payback.

"Okay, so my teammate has agreed to take care of Mika while we're gone. I'll grab her crate, and we can drop her off at his house on the way."

Emily's face falls, "Oh, I forgot we'd have to leave her. She'll be so sad." She bends over to pick up Mika, giving me a perfect view of her spectacular ass. She buries her face in Mika's fur and talks to her like a baby.

"Seriously, Emily, what is it with girls and animals and baby talk?"

"Hey, she's mine, and I can talk to her any way I want."

Point taken.

AFTER WE DROP Mika off at Alexandre's, it's a two-hour drive to the Appalachian Mountain range. The lodge I booked came highly recommended by Mackey. Like Emily said, it's his job to know these things. Why not use everything I can to make this a perfect getaway?

While I keep one eye on the road and the other on the scenery, Emily texts back and forth with Natalie. She chuckles ever so often, so it's pretty safe to assume they are talking about me.

"Everything okay back in Miami?"

"Oh, yeah, fine. Natalie says hi."

"Hi, back," I say while fussing with the radio, searching for a weather report.

"This is the Hillbilly weather guy, and I'm bringing you the real weather today. It's going to be cold as fuck later so wear your long johns," his voice booms over the car speakers.

Emily sputters. "What is that?"

"He just told you! The Hillbilly weatherman. Oh, he's a trip. He tells us what the weather is like but makes it entertaining. He covers all of New England."

"He can say the F word on the radio?"

I shrug. "Guess so."

She listens to more of the report and laughs. "Okay, he's a serious nut. I love it."

Great to hear, but how about directing some of that love my way. We're still in the early stages, and she strikes me as a woman who will let me know when she's ready to share her thoughts and feelings with me.

Fortunately, some outlet stores are on the way, and I decided to make a pit stop because I'm genuinely worried she'll freeze to death wearing what she brought from Florida.

"These snow-covered hills are majestic. What are we doing here?" she asks when I park.

"We're stopping at these stores to shop for clothes you will need for our outdoor adventure."

"Wow! Okay." She gets out, and her eyes dance with the same excitement I see in them when she holds Mika.

An hour later, she's completely outfitted for our winter adventure. She didn't want me paying, but I swipe my credit card and remind her my stock increased when I moved up to the Maulers. Plus, what's the point of having money if you can't enjoy it?

Now that she's dressed appropriately, I can no longer tease her about her choice of winter wear. I'll miss the sexy boots but she's rocking her new Uggs, hat, gloves, scarf, and puffer vest. I take a picture of her, then us. We check out the photo and she giggles so I snap a few more selfies until she's happy with the outcome.

We can't post them to social media, but I'm glad to have them anyway. We return to the Tahoe and finish our drive to the Appalachian Moose Wilderness Lodge. It's not a fancy place like you'd find in Aspen or Vail, Colorado, but all the reviews were good and said it's clean and quiet. Plus, there was Mackey's recommendation.

When we check-in for the key, I'm told we have one of the last cabins with a working fireplace. Driving to our numbered cabin, I can agree it's definitely rustic, and there's nothing fancy about it. But we're not here for the amenities, we're here for the scenery and adventure. Okay, maybe the fireplace, too.

I haul our duffle bags in and take a video of Emily pointing out the fireplace, king-size bed, and tiny bathroom like some wilderness version of Vanna White. We share a laugh and decide we should grab some quick food at the lodge. As we make our way to the restaurant, snowmobiles whiz by.

"OMG, are we going on those?" She quickly turns to me with an eager expression, waiting for an answer.

"You know you're a killjoy, right?" I mock her.

"Oh my God, we are!" she shrieks. "That's so cool. I've never been!"

And she does a cute little jig stomping her boots while she twirls in a complete circle.

"Wow!" Her little happy dance is adorable.

"Too much?" She asks as she grabs my vest and pulls herself within inches of my lips.

"You'll never be too much for me," I assure her, and our lips lock in a long steamy kiss.

After a quick but hearty chili and cornbread lunch, we make our way to the snowmobile. I showed her how to operate it and warned her to stick with me and not to follow too closely to others. I informed her it's never a good idea to deviate from the beaten path when you don't know your surroundings.

I take off first and turn my head to make sure she's still behind me when I hear a "Wahoo!"

I can't help but chuckle, and my mission has been accomplished. If a day of snowmobiling followed by a night of passionate lovemaking in front of a roaring fire doesn't make her fall in love with me, and with winter, nothing will.

20

EMILY

The trip is more than I could have ever expected. I'm beginning to see how the locals and tourists alike find so many wonderful outdoor activities even when it's below freezing outside.

We listen to Hillbilly Weatherman again and the guy cracks me up. I even looked him up on my phone. The floppy hat he wears is great, but it's his accent that really kills me. Wyatt and I share a hearty laugh as we listen to him tell us, we'll have 'cold as fuck' temperatures on the way home but if we hang around until tomorrow it will be in the high thirties.

"I can't believe you got me out in that cold!" I punch Wyatt's arm as he drives.

"But you had fun," he states, and I can't deny it. "Don't be shy with your words now, you weren't all night," he coaxes me.

I start blushing as my body immediately remembers the fire of his passion and the way it was all-consuming.

"I've never had anyone leave me breathless before."

"You demand my full focus," he comments as my phone dings.

I pull it out of the cup holder and call Natalie, who is working the golf event.

"There is a heat wave in Florida."

"How warm are we talking?"

"It's in the high eighties. But you know, this time of year. You never can tell…if a front is coming through, it can bring hot or cold air with it."

Natalie works with support staff at the links and could use my help. I've been here for close to a week and should be looking to return home.

"I should book a flight, I can do the rest of this from Miami," I say, aware that Wyatt can hear me.

"Good idea, How's the cutie?"

"Being himself," I quip.

We hang up.

He's quiet, and I can't tell if overhearing my plans to go home softened the blow or made it worse. He had to know it was coming.

"Leaving so soon?"

"I have to. I can come back up for the event; it will probably be next month."

"Sounds good," he says, but his flat tone leads me to think that he's sulking.

"Is it?" I try to read his expression as he stares at the road ahead. He gives nothing away. If anything, he's acting cold, like the first day I met him.

"I get it. I'm your job, that's all this was. You did what you came to do, and now it's time to go. Who am I to try to tell you any different? Do I wish you stayed longer? Sure." He takes his eyes off the road and fixes them on me. "I'm sure going to miss Mika."

And just like that, he delivers a sucker punch to my gut. What did he just say? He's going to miss the dog and not me? In one sentence, he lumped me into the same category as all the other women he's ever been with, even Sylvia.

He hears me gasp as all the air leaves my lungs, and like an airbag going off, I blow up.

"You mean to tell me this was – what? Just a casual fling? Did you have a side bet about getting me in bed or something?"

"No. It's just the way I see things, that's all. We have two different careers, in two different states. I don't see how this can work."

"And you're just thinking of this now?" Anger seeps into my voice, and my tone is accusatory.

This will put him on the defensive even more, but I don't care.

I'm no good at playing the 'good girl.' He can't just shit on me and expect me to be okay with it.

"I'm not a kid, and I really thought you were more mature than this." I chastise him. It's not like me to do this, and I hate myself for it, but he hurt me, dammit.

When he speaks, he sounds defeated.

"I just thought you'd never be happy here with the cold winters, and me on the road half of the season."

"You could have asked me how I felt about it instead of assuming. Don't put that on me, Wyatt."

"I didn't know I was," he shoots back bitterly.

"You can't punish me for Sylvia. You can't think all women are scheming and planning to use you. I know you don't believe that. You've been nothing but the consummate lover, especially for your age." Then I remember the only way he could be that good is to have been with quite a few ladies. But it doesn't change the fact that he just did a 180 on me.

"We had a good time, Emily. Can't that be enough?"

"Why are you running from this, from us?"

"I'm not the one who's running back to Miami! Ah, forget it, you wouldn't understand." Then he clams up.

Thankfully, we arrive back at the condo and as I am gathering up my things in the Tahoe, Wyatt's phone rings.

"Hi Dan, what's up?"

Wyatt's face turns pasty white as he listens, and he looks at me with eyes that are no longer angry. Instead, they remind me of the last day we spent together.

"What do we do?"

He listens briefly, then hands the phone to me.

"Hi, Emily. Your battery must be dead or something. I had to call Wyatt, and I'm glad he could reach you. There is a rumor you two are an item and it's hit the tabloids. Now I'm getting calls from everywhere, and the internet is blowing up. There is video footage of you taking pictures of each other at a resort…please tell me you aren't a couple," Dan pleads, but I think he already knows the truth.

"I can't do that, Dan." My voice is distant like I'm over this and don't really care what happens to Wyatt's career. That's completely unethical and so unlike me. Wyatt gives me hope that I can find someone to love me for me and that age doesn't matter.

"Damn." Dan is quiet. This scares me more than anything.

I wait and wait. Thirty seconds seems like a lifetime when your career and reputation are on the line. I've never been in this position before.

"Well, you guys are going to be in a relationship now," he commands, making me cringe. "Put me on speaker."

I hit the speaker button, and Dan's voice is past being pissed. I don't even know if there's a word for it.

"You two might have screwed up everything…unless…" he pauses.

"What?" Wyatt asks.

"We really don't want you to come off like a womanizer, Wyatt. It looks terrible. Do you have feelings for Emily?"

"Y-yea," he grumbles and looks at his feet.

"Emily?"

"Yes, even though I'm still pissed at him." I'm at a loss to understand where Dan is headed with this.

"Well, can you at least put aside your issues temporarily, or better yet fix them? You need to make this look good for media, build it up, make it look like love at first sight." I can hear the wheels in Dan's head-turning like Wyatt's fancy watch with all its moving gears.

"I'm not happy about this, Dan." I want to hide, not face the paparazzi.

"Look, Wyatt can't afford another blip. It makes him look like a fake and there are his teammates to consider. I hate to play this card, but you can't represent him anymore. I'll handle things from here on out. You two go out in public, act like it's all fucking fantastic in real life, and try to sort things out."

He hangs up.

Fuck.

I glare at Wyatt as we walk in silence through the garage and to the elevator. Taking this route, we don't walk by Mackey.

My mind is going in circles trying to figure out how anyone would know where we were to get that footage. Only one person knew where we were going: Mackey. He must be behind the leak – and suddenly, I wonder if he had something to do with Sylvia, too.

"What time was Sylvia at your condo?"

"Late. Like, two a.m.."

"What time did she leave?"

"Early, she had a nine o'clock morning class and had to go home first. Why?"

We enter his apartment to find that his friend has already dropped the puppy off for us. I'm so happy to see Mika, I hunch down and let her hop in my lap as she knocks me over, licking my face, and I curl into a ball. Even with all the shit going on, I'm laughing, as she's funny and adorable, and her rough tongue tickles.

When I've recovered, I put her leash on her and pause at the door.

"I think you might have someone close to you who sold us out," I say, opening the door to take Mika out. "Did you tell anyone that we were going to be at the lodge? Because if you didn't, Mackey is the only person who knew. You said he recommended it to you, right?"

"Yeah. He does that for everyone. He's lived here forever."

"Interesting," I say as I head down the hall to the elevator.

Mika and I walk past Mackey in the lobby at the concierge desk. I wonder if he's responsible for turning our lives upside down. He may do more for money than his job here pays. He might have a side gig selling juicy inside information to the press. If Mackey was looking for low-hanging fruit, Wyatt, being the latest rookie and a hot commodity, was ripe for the picking.

Now that it's warming up and the snow is starting to melt, I can play outside with Mika longer than usual. It's in the forties today, and the roads are wet with melting snow. Now, if only I could get this warming trend to thaw Wyatt's attitude.

He disengaged immediately after he heard I planned to fly home. There wasn't even a discussion. Doesn't he realize we're in the 21st century, where women work and travel and still have relationships?

Imagine that. I haven't heard much about his family, but something flipped a switch in him, and now we are stuck together again.

I hear a car door slamming and when I glance down the road, I find cars and a van lined up along the main road. Fuck! The press is here.

I've never been party to a media frenzy like this and I'm afraid that Wyatt's future may be in jeopardy once again.

Here, I thought we'd just be able to hop on a plane and return in a few weeks, while Wyatt and I got to know each other better.

All bets are off now. I pick my dog up and hurry back inside.

"Wyatt." I burst into the condo. "The media is at the gate!"

"That's not good. You came here to save my career, not decimate it!"

"I didn't," I shout back. "I did fix it, and I asked if you were sure about taking the next step, and for a few days, you were fantastic. Then, I mention flying home and you freaked out."

Again, his answer is to turn his back, open the refrigerator, and pull out food that looks like it might make dinner.

"You're eating in a time like this?"

"Hockey players always eat." He goes through the leftovers, clearly weighing his options.

"Fuck it. Let's give the media a show; the sooner we give them what they want, the sooner they'll be off our case," I say in frustration.

"Fine, I know just the place. It's on the water. Some of the guys are there tonight with their wives. You'll have to get sexed up. I'll call some guys and see who wants to meet up."

"Fine." I stomp off towards his room, with no time to move my stuff to the guest room, but I want no part of him if he's going to be so immature.

I shower and slip into my suit, adding a sexier top for the afternoon get-together.

I slip into my black Christian Louboutin pumps that I wore for the business meeting earlier this week.

I'd rather have a nap; all the stress is wearing me out, and I'm not in the best of moods.

"We've got to get you something else to wear," Wyatt comments when I leave the bedroom.

"What do you mean by that? You're so critical of everything I wear, yet you can't answer any of my questions. Why do I care?"

"Because the press will follow us, and you have to make it look like you belong and you're one of us, and that outfit will not cut it. You need to show off more cleavage and something tighter to show off your body."

"You've got to be kidding me," spills out of my mouth before I can stop it. Of course, that's how it is. I'm not dressed like all the player's wives and girlfriends who stroll through our Miami and New York offices.

Dan got me into his, well, I had a hand in that I guess, but he's trying to get us out. The least I can do is play the game for the next 24 hours, which is usually how long it takes for the press to move on to something else.

"Fine, let's go shopping, but I'm not happy about it." I grab my purse.

21

WYATT

What is it with me and the girls this year? Either I'm the unluckiest guy on the planet at keeping my personal life private or Emily is on to something regarding her suspicions about Mackey. To test her theory, we say goodbye to him and let him know we are leaving for the evening and that we'll be at the Bay Side Country Club. If our suspicions are correct, he'll call his media connection when we're out of earshot.

We still need to get her something to wear, so we drive to the mall where Emily makes a beeline to a store selling formal wear. Once inside, she grabs an armful of cocktail dresses off the rack and heads to the dressing room.

I can tell she's upset, but I'm not sure if it's over me or Mackey. Either way, it's unsettling she's not in a mood to smile.

Now I understand why it bothers her when I'm elusive and don't talk about my thoughts and feelings. I keep it in, always have, and rarely talk about my private life, even with the guys.

Tristan is probably the one I would call if I needed to talk. I got a text from Mac the other day for a pick-up game, but I don't want to risk an injury while playing pond hockey. That would fuck my career up faster than my girl problems.

Then I have Alexandre, an egotistical bastard, but he's been good to me. I wouldn't want to be the woman who dates him. He's the hot shot on the team, and his ego arrives on the ice before he does, but he's given me great advice, and I enjoy his company.

Emily interrupts my thoughts, coming out of the dressing room wearing a shimmery dress that clings to her curves and accentuates her hourglass figure. She looks prettier than the runway models I see on TV as she stands in front of the mirror and smooths the material over her perfect body.

She's worried about fitting in with the hockey wives and girl-friends. Little does she know, she has what it takes to pull this off. The only difference is- the other girls would be upset if a puppy or kid got that dress dirty and bitch about it all night. Emily never would.

Emily has completely disproved my first assumption that she's high-maintenance.

"That's more like it," I say, wanting to tell her she's a knockout but saving that for another time. I haven't been in the pros long, but I know that it's an NHL fashion show with or without music when they go out. "We'll take it," I confirm what she's probably thinking. It's gorgeous. "You do like it, don't you?"

"Oh.," She fumbles with the tag. "This is not in my budget. Maybe the clearance rack?" she suggests.

"You need better shoes, too."

"These are designers," she scoffs.

"Well, whatever you want, but I'm telling you, they need to scream sex and money."

"Great," she huffs and heads to the shoe department, still wearing the shimmering dress.

While she looks at stilettos, I pick out a black Prada clutch and a thick gold bangle to complete the look.

"I think these are for younger girls. My feet are already killing me," she grumbles as she walks back and forth to test the fit and check the look in the full-length mirror.

So, this is what women go through all the time.

It's more work for women than us.

"We'll take them," I say, glancing at my watch to see the time. "It's a later crowd, so we're fine. The important thing was to find you something to wear. Now you're dressed like my girlfriend, not my public relations expert or an agent."

Without removing the dress, Emily has the cashier scan and remove her price tags. There's nothing more for me to do than hold her coat and swipe my credit card while we both chuckle. It's nice to laugh with her again and lift our dark moods.

Back in the car, she flips down the visor and opens the lighted mirror to apply red lipstick. Her nails are also a bright red but look natural, not acrylic.

She asks, "How are we on time?"

"Fine, we can relax now. So, what's the plan when we get there? Are you going to bite my head off again?"

"I'm sorry I lost it. I'm just frustrated and angry and.." looking out her window, "I'm not myself right now."

And for a minute, her voice softens, so soft I wonder if she is okay.

We're not married or officially dating, and yet, we're being hounded by the press. As a result, our budding relationship is now under a microscope and strained by the added attention when we're not at our best. How do other players handle this daily?

"I don't know how to do this. I'm sorry," I say, glancing at her as she wipes a tear from her cheek and changes items from her old purse to her new Prada clutch.

"I know, me too."

She's rubbing her fingers over the new bracelet, and it reminds me of the spinner toy kids play with to eliminate anxiety. She told me days ago that she likes her desk job and some travel, but she never asked to be in the spotlight.

"What do we do when we get there?"

"I hold your hand, we act happy, smile, and kiss, I guess. Once we're inside, you'll meet my friends and players. There will be other girls there," I reassure her. She's out of her element, and I love her and want to make her comfortable.

I want her to not hate this, me, or the cold. I thought I was doing well until she announced she was going back to Florida. My head was in the clouds, high on love, and returning to reality was such a hard fall. I feel like I failed.

We're quiet on our short ride to the club, and when we get there, I pull up front and hand my keys to the valet. I walk around to her side and take her hand as she steps out of the car. We smile at each other just as the horde of the photographers and the media with microphones stampede towards us.

"It's *Hockey Scoop* magazine, which is like the *TMZ* of the hockey world," I whisper in her ear.

"There's a hockey magazine for stuff like this," she says in amazement.

"Exactly, let's kiss and turn around–play it up. Let's have fun, Emily," I plead, wishing so much we could return to the ski lodge and the road trip before everything went wrong.

She lifts her chin. Her eyes flicker with deceit or love. I can't tell which.

"Let's do this." She smiles and winks.

In full view of the cameras, I lean down and pull her into my arms, planting my mouth on hers. Pent-up emotions take over, and our contrived kiss turns into a deep, lingering tongue bath that makes me forget we're not alone.

Her lips push back on mine with desire. My heart fills with her warmth. We pull apart to pose for the cameras and try to look surprised so it doesn't look like we knew they'd be here.

Emily and I flash our red carpet smiles, and I feel confident we're dressed for the red carpet. Reporters shout out questions like "Where did you meet? How long have you been dating?"

I wave and guide Emily inside the private club where the press can't follow us.

"You know what this means?"

"What? That we're like the popular couple for the week?"

"Well, they'll be digging to find out who I am. But, no." She taps the arm I've threaded through hers. "It means Mackey is on the take. He sold us out. It's probably not the first time."

"Right, well, I told Dan about your theory, and the building management is going to look into it this week. I doubt he'll be there much longer," I say, knowing my career is the only thing keeping me from kicking his ass all over that lobby.

"Oh, how is he, by the way?"

"Great." I smile down at her, and it's as if our little tiff never happened. We've stopped talking about the issues, but they never went away. They're just hiding behind the smiles we wear.

I spot Alexandre leaning against the bar, wearing a colorful suit that reminds me of a peacock. I'm just getting to know him, and so far, he's quite the character.

We do the common fist bump. Sometimes, we bring it in, but not tonight.

"Alexandre, Emily." I introduce them, and they shake hands.

"Nice to see you both here. Rumor has it that the press was outside. Have any idea what that's about? Are you back on the naughty list? Because we can't have that. We just won and we need to keep it going if we want to give Toronto a run to the finish. Besides, I want a crack at the President's Trophy."

"I know, but that trophy is bad luck, man; I'd rather be in second place and not worry about the bad juju."

"Maybe." He shrugs before picking up his whisky drink from the bar. "Well, at any rate, I need more TOI."

"You have plenty of time on the ice," I flippantly respond.

"No, more time on Irene," he casually replies, looking over my shoulder. I turn to see he's watching a supermodel-looking woman approaching us.

"Get it? More Time On Irene," he says, laughing at his joke. He finishes his whiskey and slaps my upper arm. "That's Irene."

"Oh." This must be his new girl. Leave it to Alexandre to have a unique flavor every week.

I shake my head as I watch him intercept her, whisper in her ear, and take her by the arm to circulate the room.

"That was quick," Emily comments as she pulls her phone out and checks the internet.

"Maybe you should save that for later," I'm about to take her phone and put it in her bag. "If not, it could ruin your night."

Having been through this once, I'm better equipped to handle the sequel.

"How will the GM take this?" she nervously asks.

"Better than the other incident. This is the normal kind of stuff, the dating, when you have a new girlfriend, and the press and fans are curious. It's not that uncommon."

"You talk like you've done this before."

"I did have a few smaller incidents in Europe, and I've been around guys that dated popular women, so, yeah. Some of this is normal," and I lift an eyebrow to see if she's cool with this, but she says nothing.

"Let's circulate," I suggest, retaking her arm while she puts her phone in her purse.

She's uncomfortable, trying to figure out how to carry her new clutch, and when I sneak a peek at her, she looks overwhelmed. Her eyes are enormous, taking in her surroundings and everyone in there. This is her first experience with the team players looking like they stepped off the pages of *GQ,* and the women are so *Vogue.*

There are cliques of girls standing around tables, and the guys hang out at the bar while others mingle. This is Sunday night when the team gets together at least twice a month.

"You can call this a team builder. Our captain, Victor Karlsson, is big on us doing things together," I explain.

"I think that's good. Who are those women over there?"

"Those are the player's girlfriends. I heard chatter that the wives and girlfriends aren't all friends."

"I've read about it online and saw it on that new reality show I've been watching on YouTube."

"Never heard of it. Remember why we're here. We have to sell it to the team, too."

"Right, forgot about that," and her eyes dart around the room like a caged animal. "Where should we sit?"

"Anywhere. I don't know the guys well, so we're in the same boat," and when she looks up at me, I take the opportunity to give her an encouraging kiss before we continue moving about the room.

"I wonder what's for dinner," she asks. "I see a carving station."

"Oh, don't worry, there will be plenty of surf and turf, trust me. Can I get you a cocktail?"

"Sure, a Cosmo, please."

I leave her to get us drinks and see Luc at the bar. "Cute girl, Wyatt."

"Thanks, I'm sorry about the whole thing with Sylvia."

"I'm sorry too, I overreacted. She can be …difficult. She can't get enough attention, and she acts out. I'm sorry you were sucked into the drama. No hard feelings."

"Thanks." I turn back to Emily and see a teammate about her age chatting her up.

It's nice to see everyone so accommodating, but I wonder if Emily might be more interested in someone closer to her age. Now that she's gotten past lumping all athletes together in a disparaging way, she just opened the door to the candy store.

22

EMILY

I'm standing next to Wyatt, wearing clothes that make me feel like a million bucks, but I'm not used to any of this. Outside of work, I haven't been to anything purely social in so long, I forgot what it feels like.

I also haven't been on a date in so long, that holding hands and having my doors opened for me feels weird. My insecurities surface and the part of me that's been burned in the past, whispers in my ear, warning me this won't last. Unable to ignore the voices in my head, I wonder how long it will be before he no longer wants me. How long before he shuts me out again?

I can't understand Wyatt's frosty attitude and his wall of silence after he found out I was flying home. It's not like I'm never coming back. We have the Celebrity Skate fundraiser to attend. Sure, I could have talked to him about leaving, but I didn't think I needed to go over all my plans with him.

The silent treatment knocked me for a loop. I've heard of men like this. They keep it all bottled up, afraid to show any vulnerability. But if I'm going to be his girlfriend or partner, he needs to be open with me and articulate his feelings. I'm no mind reader.

While Wyatt gets me a Cosmo, I'm approached by a man

who introduces himself as Victor, the team captain. He's taller than Wyatt and just as good-looking. He tells me about growing up in Michigan when I feel Wyatt's eyes watching me. A minute later, Wyatt joins us and slides his arm around my waist. Victor is polite and excuses himself to talk to others.

Wyatt has to have feelings for me, otherwise, why would he cock block the conversation? It's cute how he subtly stakes his claim, but I won't change my life for a man I've known less than a month. I'm keeping my options open.

I sip my Cosmo and look at my new bracelet. It's beautiful and the only piece of jewelry anyone has ever given me. Everything I own, I bought. I feel bad letting him spend his hard-earned money when I could try to expense this through Dan. But I couldn't be the one to crush Wyatt's happiness when he whipped out his platinum card and paid for everything. He likes to spoil me, and I must admit, I like it.

At dinner, I listen to everyone and try to figure out who is who. By the time ten o'clock rolls around, the group is breaking up. They have a game tomorrow, and thankfully it's a home game.

We bid our good nights and head to the valet. Even though Wyatt is new, there is already a bond with his teammates. The women, well, I'm not so sure. They have their cliques. I was not invited to join any of them. They probably need to see me at a lot more of these functions before they accept me into their circle of trust. None of them asked for my number or suggested lunch. I didn't expect special treatment

My life does not depend on hanging out with a catty bunch of women. If I can make friends with one or two who I can sit with at the games, I'll call that a success.

I'm sleepy by the time we get back to the condo. It's been a long day and I'm emotionally drained as well. Wyatt offers to take Mika out and while he's gone, I think about whether or not I should stay.

He's been in such a weird mood, maybe I'd be better off at my hotel room.

When he returns with Mika, I still have not made a decision. Instead, I'm organizing the clothes I left strewn all over his room.

"You okay?" I ask, folding my bra and panties.

"Yeah, no. I mean, shit's fucked up a bit." I hear him take a deep breath and brace for a breakup speech.

"Sorry about my mood. When I saw Victor chatting you up tonight, I felt something I never felt with anyone else." He sits on the end of the bed and watches me continue to fuss with my clothes.

He stops me by placing his hand on top of mine and says, "I'm not the jealous type but for the first time I felt territorial when I saw you smiling and laughing with him. I don't know Victor well but he's a great captain and if you'd like to date him, I'll step aside."

If I had been drinking my usual mocha frappe, I would have choked on it. I haven't missed my expensive morning habit since I've been staying with Wyatt and making new concoctions with his coffee machine

"What do you mean, date Victor?" I interject and plop down next to him.

"I thought you might like him….he's more your age," he says quietly while mindlessly picking dog hair off his shirt sleeve.

"We've never talked about the future. We've been in this bubble, this perfect bubble." I make a circle with my hands. "But I don't want anyone but you, Wyatt. The problem is, I don't know what you want. Do you want me? Do you want kids?"

"Yes, to wanting you, in fact, my cock just got hard thinking about you, and yes, I want kids, eventually. I mean, we work well together, and traveling with you is great. You get into the adventure and roll with the unexpected even when you're hungry." He gives me that devilish grin I love.

Taking my hand, he places it in his lap so I can feel his hard cock through his dress pants. I massage it just a bit but the man needs no foreplay. He's always ready to go.

He leans in and whispers against my neck, "Maybe Mackey did us a favor."

Our eyes meet. I'm growing warmer by the second and my thin panties are soaked just thinking about how sexy he looks when he's on top of me. When he slides his thick cock inside of me, there's no better feeling in the world.

"We went out tonight because we had to and it served our purpose. Speaking of which—" I break eye contact with him and his hotness, to crawl across the bed and grab my new purse.

"What are you doing?" he asks as he stands to undress.

"Checking my phone, occupational hazard. Didn't I mention, I work too much?"

"I gathered that on my own. Why do you think I make love to you all the time and spend my late mornings lazing around with you? I thought you'd catch on by now," he says while pulling me by the feet back towards him.

"I'm not the prolific dater you seem to think I am. I'm pretty smart but it comes at a price," unlocking my phone with one hand and pulling off my heels with the other.

Flipping through social media sites, I'm on the lookout for postings with our picture. I finally found the pictures taken in front of the country club, and we look adorable. I want to contact the photographer and get copies. The picture where Wyatt kisses me-totally believable- that we're in love.

But when I read the comments under the photo, I gasped like I just fell through the ice at the hockey pond.

"What is it?" Wyatt leans over my shoulder to see my phone. "What?"

"This one says I look too old for you and the next one is talking about how you can't keep it in your pants."

"Haters gonna hate," he states, and as much as I appreciate his rise-above-it attitude, these people are judging us and accusing Wyatt of things he hasn't done. They don't even know us.

"I wouldn't look at it, people can be cruel. Opinions are like assholes, everyone has one."

"But, it affects us."

"No, it doesn't. Only if you let it."

"And you don't?"

"If it was career-ending, sure, like the Sylvia thing. But the fact that we're seeing each other and we're both adults, it's off-limits."

"Some think we're off-limits." I look back at my phone.

"Some will, no matter what. As long as we're not breaking the law, it's just opinions and speculations. And remember, people troll those sites as well."

He's right, there will always be losers hiding behind their keyboards who want to stir the pot and spread their negative agenda.

"Are you okay with me being a cradle robber? Oh, this one wants to know, who's the gold digger!" I exclaim.

He answers me with a resounding kiss, that I eagerly accept, and it leads to more. I'm happy for the distraction.

I hear the *Ballers* ring tone and we both know it's Dan calling me.

"Dan, what's up?"

"The internet is blowing up about you two. I saw the photos and the comments. You didn't have to sacrifice yourself and the next few months of your life in order to get the press off the question of his healthy scratch."

A healthy scratch is when a player is taken out of play for the game due to a punishment or other reason that is not related to an injury.

"It's all good, Dan." I put him on speaker.

"Oh, and Mackey won't be returning to work. It turns out he tends to change jobs, moving around and working in places with access to stars. I guess he needed a big payday, and, taking advantage of the recent rumblings in the press, he cashed in on the new kid."

"Well, ain't that some shit," Wyatt comments as he nibbles on my ear and unzips my dress.

"Are you still going to help with the Celebrity Skate fundraiser? In about six weeks, I'll be able to get around without crutches. The fundraiser is in April. The weather will be warmer. The projected turnout is looking good."

"Well, sure. Why wouldn't I? I'm fine with you representing Wyatt. Now that there is no conflict of interest, my job here is done."

"Ha, you sure went above and beyond, Emily. But if you're happy, I'm happy."

"Right now, I'm very happy." I stifle my giggle as Wyatt starts licking between my legs, his tongue soft and moist, going higher and higher as I fall back on the pillows. Crotchless underwear, what a concept.

23

WYATT

"Emily, why don't you just give up your hotel room?"

"Hmm, that's a nice offer, but I don't know."

"It's not like you go there anyway. There's no way I want you to stay there alone, and you can't take Mika with you. She'd cry all night without you here," I try my best at insisting. "It makes sense."

"I know..."

"Okay," I come around the kitchen counter, checking out her cute butt in a team tracksuit with our Moose logo. She looks adorable. I want to see her in my home every day.

"This isn't very romantic, but I'm asking it now anyway. Emily, please move in with me," and I wrap my arms around her from behind and I peer over her shoulder as she stirs homemade spaghetti sauce. The aroma of fresh tomatoes, basil, and parsley makes me hungry.

"Well, how can I refuse when you put it like that?"

"Great! I'll clear out some space in my closet for all that stuff you piled on my dresser," I tease. She whips her head around to give me a look that could turn anyone to stone.

"Just kidding," I shout over my shoulder as I head to my

bedroom to move some of my winter crap to the other bedroom's closet.

And just like that, we're dating and living together.

"What is the date of that fundraiser?"

"It's after Easter. Everyone will be in town, and the season is still going on," she hollers back.

"Great." I walk into the kitchen and pet Mika. In the two weeks she's been here, she's gained a few pounds and grown a few inches.

"I have a meeting at the arena tomorrow," she says while straining the spaghetti noodles.

This woman knows the way to my heart is cooking. Well, that and all the other naughty things I'd like to do with her involving food.

"Really?"

"Yes, we're tying up loose ends, reviewing the fundraising letter, and doing a final rundown of everything. It has to be on a Saturday or Sunday. The team doesn't have a game since we're using the rink and arena. The players will give out autographs, paid for of course."

"That's too bad. So many kids would love that experience, and it's still expensive."

"I know, but it's raising money for a good cause. Let's not forget this is a long time coming since that ordeal with you and Sylvia happened weeks ago. And by the way, Dan hopes he can make it to this fundraiser. He's doing well with the rehab on the leg."

"Good to hear that," I say, moving here and there around the kitchen, almost like a dance, to get what's needed to set the table for two.

"Just think, if it weren't for his accident, we wouldn't have met."

"True, how about that? And to think I was going to join a dating app, as much as I hate them."

"Their loss, my gain," I say, wrapping my arms around her. "I like winning."

"I know," she says, kissing me.

"Did you feed Mika?"

"No, I forgot. I'm a bad mommy; no wonder she keeps looking at me," Emily says as she dips a spoon in the sauce, blows on it, and gives it a taste test. "We'll live," she deadpans.

"Aww, come on, you're a great cook."

She lifts the bottle of red wine we're having with dinner and pours some into the sauce. "That ought to do it." She stirs and, when she's satisfied, spreads large meatballs over pasta before adding the sauce.

Delivering the two plates of spaghetti to the dining room table, she says, "I need to go home at some point. Should I go before the fundraiser or after?"

"How about never," I tease, it may sound like I'm kidding, but I'm not.

"Ha, forever is a long time. If I had houseplants, they'd be dead by now. You're lucky that I don't have anything tying me down. In fact, that might be the main reason I was sent here. I'm the one at the office with the least number of commitments."

I can tell this is an epiphany for her.

She looks at me, a bit freaked out. "I wonder if I'll remember my place, surroundings, routine. I just picked up and left; it's a bit surreal."

I lean over and kiss her before she can take a bite. "It's fine, sweetie, don't stress."

I grab the bottle of red and fill our crystal wine glasses three-quarters of the way.

Emily lifts the glass to her nose and inhales gently, breathing in the aroma, "Fruity, maybe chocolate?"

"Yes, boy, you're good at this."

"Ha, I worked as a waitress in an upscale restaurant before law school. Some skills are hard-wired," she muses and sips, letting it roll in her mouth before swallowing.

I love watching her do this. My cock is as hard as a hockey puck remembering the last time we had a date night, and we slipped wine into each other's mouth when nobody was looking. It felt a bit dirty-but I loved it. The risk of getting caught being too sexual in an eating establishment made it extra exciting.

"Hmm, that's good, huh? Too bad spaghetti is best eaten hot. Otherwise, I'd suggest we eat later." I sip my wine and suggestively lick my lips, just enough to let her know what I'm thinking.

"Oh, Wyatt, we can do the dishes much later."

"You read my mind."

EMILY FELL ASLEEP, and I lay awake, worried about her condo in Florida and her job. More importantly, I wish I had some assurance that she doesn't mind the age gap and that she can handle life here or wherever I might end up. Chances are high we will always live in cold weather states, but there is a chance that I could play on a team based in the south. It's not like the 1970s when all hockey was played in states with cold winters.

Sure, we had to deal with the press occasionally, but we make it a point not to look for that news. It will be quite a while before I'm asked to participate with family photos on the team's social media account. I'm still the new guy, the inconsequential player, and I'll enjoy my privacy for as long as possible.

If I continue to do my job well, I'll eventually be in the limelight, and we'll be together. I don't know if Emily has thought about it, but we must start planning our next move. We're in love, but it's better to pull the rip cord sooner rather than later if you know there is no future.

I hope she'll be happy enough to live with me. But sometimes, people make promises, and love isn't enough when reality hits.

24

EMILY

I'm walking into the arena for my last face-to-face to go over all the final details we've been working on for the week. Things are looking up for the team as they are in the first wild card slot and there is still time for them to move into fourth place for the playoffs.

I've been ordering things I need because I didn't pack much and never expected to be here for two weeks. As they say, time flies when you're having fun.

I walk into the conference room and there are new faces. More women than normal. It's obvious they aren't staff, judging by their clothing and the bling on their fingers. I rack my brain trying to figure out why they look familiar. But I can't quite place it.

"Hi, Emily." Mr. Devonshire looks handsome in his dark blue power suit.

I take his hand. "Mr. Devonshire."

"Call me Gary, please."

"Okay, Gary I see we have more people today?"

"Oh, yes, these are some of the wives of players and the wife of the General Manager, Mary Price, is here. Since this fundraiser is so important to her husband, she's here to give her input. There are a few wives as well who want to help," he smiles and I'm not sure if it's a real smile or pasted on like dried milk- like mine.

"Oh, how lovely." I fake enthusiasm because I'm seeing red. I doubt these women are really that committed. Mary is the exception because this is her husband's favorite charity event. That's why I chose a Celebrity Skate, it ensured they'd be onboard when I needed to get Wyatt on their good side.

Now I'm beginning to see our public relations stunt worked on numerous fronts. The downside is, we were outed as a couple before we would have liked. The upside is, we no longer have to live in the shadows.

I wish Wyatt was here, but he has training, and I can't expect him to hold my hand just because I'm out of my comfort zone. I have to man up and swallow my fear of these potential barracudas.

I take a deep breath as I walk across the large conference room. Status and hierarchy have to be acknowledged, so I introduce myself to Mary first.

"Oh, hello, dear." She extends a hand that looks frail and much older than her face. She's pretty with grey-blue eyes and straight silver hair that is perfectly cut and lays flat, framing her heart-shaped face.

"Hello, Mrs. Price, such a pleasure to meet you." I take her tiny hand in mine.

"Thank you so much for your time, and it's so nice to meet you, truly. My boss Dan is a friend of your husband."

"Oh, that's so nice. I appreciate your help. I hear you do an excellent job with your golf fundraisers. Jon just loves going to the one in Miami every year."

"It's fun, and he gets a week of sun!" She seems harmless enough.

I figure if Dan likes her husband, they must be nice people.

"I don't know anyone else here. Who are the women over

there?" and I subtly cock my head towards the gaggle of women standing by the windows.

"Oh, that's Justin Puljujar's wife Charlie. She's a former model who retired to have kids. He's one of our defensemen. I'm not sure about the others, but I doubt any girlfriends would be here, so they must be wives."

"Thank you, I'll say a quick hello, and then I guess it's time to start the meeting."

"You run along, dear." Her genuine smile makes me feel welcome, and for that, I'm grateful.

"Thank you." I take my leave.

I'm so glad I bought a new suit and that I didn't take any short-cuts with my hair and makeup this morning. Women can be so critical.

"Hello, ladies." I force a smile and think I'm doing well until Charlie Pjljujar turns to me. "Thank you for the opportunity to help with the Celebrity Skate. I've proposed it numerous times but never got anywhere. You must teach me your secret." She extends a hand dripping with diamonds. "Charlie, nice to meet you, Emily, you're quite the talk around here."

"I have no idea if that's true." I recover from my nervousness.

The other women introduce themselves. The meeting starts as soon as I grab some coffee. It's not nearly as good as the coffee I get out of Wyatt's coffee machine.

The meeting went well. Everything is set for a day in April, and I stop in the women's bathroom to relieve myself of the coffee I drank. While I'm in there, I hear the girls come in.

"You know, she's older than him, he'll be banging some young puck bunny in no time. Besides, she's just never going to fit in here. She's from Miami, it's like a different country. I don't see her giving up the nightlife and excitement there for Maine of all places. At least my husband is here for a limited contract, I have the opportunity to move to another state. Wyatt is young, he might spend his entire career here. If he can keep his dick in his pants, that is."

"Yeah, I don't know. My husband and I are the same age so we're pretty much on the same page. We enjoy the same music, y'know. How old do you think she is?"

Another voice chimes in. "She's pretty, I'll give her that. She's educated, but Wyatt's too young to get married, and her ovaries aren't getting any younger. You wouldn't believe how many women over thirty have fertility issues."

They run the water after they pee and wash their hands while I remain hidden in my stall until they leave.

They aren't wrong. I never expected to fall in love with anyone, let alone Wyatt. But he's a sweetheart, and I'd be happy to have him for my husband. I just don't know what I'd do for work. Maybe being an agent as a satellite office for Dan wouldn't be so bad after all.

The one thing I'm sure of, I cannot pretend to like these bitches.

25

WYATT

Emily isn't the same after her meeting at the arena. I try getting details out of her, but she's acting like me, sullen and withdrawn. She says she's fine, but she's not.

"Who all was at that meeting?"

"Just some wives. The GM's wife was nice.

"I heard that about her."

"How was practice?"

"Great. We're starting to gel, so I hope we'll do well in our next game."

"I'm sure you will. You have a great group of guys.

"True."

"So, how long do you think you'll be playing for this team?"

"I have no idea. Why do you ask?"

She shrugs as she reaches for the TV remote. Mika is getting too big to curl up in her lap but seems content to snuggle next to her on the couch.

"This life is unpredictable, and sometimes it's like joining the Army in that regard."

"What do you want to watch?"

"I don't care."

My phone goes off. It's Tristan.

"Hey dude, how the hell are you?" I take the call into the den so I don't bother Emily.

"Long time, man," he says. I listen to him talk, and he's got a new girlfriend. I tell him about Emily, and he saw the pictures of us but can't believe she's almost ten years older than me, and he's like, man, sometimes love doesn't know age.

"True, I'm just not sure she'll be happy with me down the road. I mean, our lives are dictated by my career. She might get tired of me; she has nothing tying her down anywhere. It's a big risk."

"Wyatt, you've never run from a challenge. Don't try to predict how she'll react to a life with you. If you have all these concerns, it sounds like you're both talking, but you're not really communicating."

"That's a fair point, Tristan."

After about ten more minutes of hockey talk, I say goodbye and return to Emily, who has fallen asleep on the couch.

She won't tell me what happened today, but something changed.

TED MACKEY WAS FIRED, and there are no plans to have him replaced. With the money the condo association is saving, we voted to use it to buy some new gym equipment and renovate the dry spa.

With the weather is warming up. Emily is taking Mika on a nice long walk and getting her used to a harness leash.

When I hear them come inside, I holler from the kitchen, "Are you coming to my game tonight?" I assume she'll say yes since she's here and not busy.

"Sure, I wouldn't miss it," she quips, taking off Mika's leash and hanging it by the door on a rack she bought, and I nailed it to the wall. It was the first thing I added that didn't come with the place and felt good.

She follows Mika into the kitchen. "You didn't sound very convincing. Is everything okay?"

"Oh.," She shrugs. "I don't know what to do. The women at the meeting the other day were not kind. I don't know how I'll ever fit in with them. Honestly, I don't want to fit in with them. They're just a bunch of mean girls."

"Life isn't always unicorns and rainbows. We have jobs, and they aren't always easy. There will be days when it's tough, and we have to deal with several different personalities, some downright sinister, not all of them pretty."

"Tell me about it." She sighs and rolls her eyes.

"I understand it's overwhelming now, but it won't continue forever. You're not a teenage girl. They may act like it, but you can't let them win. Do you think it's easy for me to ignore the nasty comments when an opponent is trying to draw a penalty in my ear?" I point out. "No, it's never easy, but I get to do what I love and love you. I choose you. Look, we didn't let the press break us up or the fact that you live in a different state. In fact, you're still here working on the fundraiser when you didn't have to be here, so I know you love me too."

"I do love you, Wyatt. But I have a job. It's what I do, and it's because of my job that I'm still here."

She comes over to where I'm sitting on the huge island in the kitchen. We eat most of our meals here, so it brings back a lot of fond memories.

She pulls out a bar stool and sits, leaning in to kiss me. Mika follows her and flops down next to our chairs. She always wants to be near Emily; I know how she feels.

Emily speaks first. "I don't know if I can play their games. I don't want to get that involved."

"You can't mean that. You could have gone home and come back in April. Or you could have delegated your work here to someone else and never returned."

She can try and deny it, but the truth is, she chose to be here, to be with me.

"I love you, and we can work it out. We can work through anything."

"Maybe it's too late for me. I've never had any luck with boyfriends, and I've only had a few girlfriends my entire life. I guess I'm just a loner."

"So am I."

"No, I don't believe that for one minute. You are not a loner," she stands up. "You've been in sports your entire life, and you've traveled. I don't even like to go to New York."

"This isn't New York. Don't you want more? We can live here and be happy. You have to give it a chance."

"I'll think about it. What time is your game?"

"I need to go. I'll leave you a ticket at will call. The wives and girlfriends have a box tonight. Please make it. You might be pleasantly surprised."

"I'll be at the game, but I don't know if I will be happy with the girls."

"Well, I have to go." I stand, and Mika jumps around my feet and tries to undo the shoelaces in my sneakers. "You are such a cute dog." I rub her head and pick up the ball lying near her. I throw it, and she returns, chewing it and making it squeak.

She follows on my heels while I grab my coat and keys.

Emily is standing in the kitchen, her arms crossed, looking pensive.

"I'll watch you play."

"I know you will."

26

EMILY

I know Wyatt's right, but at my age, I'm not sure I can change. Whereas men have a tendency to avoid change, I'm even worse. That's why I've been at my current job so long and holed up in the same condo for years.

I'm afraid to put myself out there and risk the agony of defeat when people reject or hurt me. I trust only a handful of people. It would be difficult for me to participate in a large group activity without Wyatt by my side. He's the fearless one.

I don't work law cases that could potentially go to trial because I avoid the limelight, preferring to work behind the scenes. To be on display makes me vulnerable, like taking the shell off a turtle. It's easier for me to hide behind a desk than it is to get in front of it.

But a promise is a promise, and I love Wyatt more than I hate my fear. I'll go to the game. If I don't like the girls, I'll move.

I need to get ready, so I shower and do my hair, putting it up like the day I met Wyatt at the pond. I can't believe how tired and frustrated I was that day. But when our eyes met, the sparks flew, and none of the other stuff mattered.

I can try to change for the sake of love. I don't know if it will make me happy, but Wyatt makes me happy, and Mika is our little bonus. If it wasn't for her, I don't know if I'd be standing here right now.

I have no clue how the other girls will dress, but I'm dressing to my standards, not theirs. Tonight, it's not work, it's a pleasure, and I plan to watch my boyfriend play in a great game, and I won't let anyone take that from me.

I pull on a pair of my Lucky jeans and hope they bring me luck. Expecting it to be cold in the arena, I layer a short sleeve with a long-sleeved t-shirt and throw on one of Wyatt's jerseys.

Tugging on my thigh-high leather boots, I critique my look in front of the floor-to-ceiling mirror in the dining room.

"What do you think, Mika? Do I look like a hockey fan or a sexy swashbuckler?"

She jumps on my legs, and I pick her up. I won't be able to do this much longer. Holding her in my arms, it dawned on me that she melted my heart and let love in; she was the sticky glue that bonded me and Wyatt. Well, that and our hot physical connection that, for the life of me, I can't explain.

He's more than just smoking hot; he's intelligent and determined, and I'm sure he had to work harder than me to get where he is. If anything, he shows me what can be accomplished when we put our minds to something.

I put Mika down and called Natalie.

"Hey girl, heading out to the game."

"Awesome, are you calling to ask me to be a bridesmaid? You've been sequestered in your love nest for over two weeks. Are you coming back or staying?"

I let out a nervous laugh. She's so wise for her age, but I guess growing up with parents who snorted their entire inheritance up their noses and left her alone most of the time does that to a kid.

"You're so smart, Natalie. I have a question for you."

"Shoot."

"Do you think Wyatt, at nineteen, can decide what he wants for the rest of his life?"

"Does it matter? What is your idea of success? Going to the beach every Sunday by yourself? Do you want to play it safe your entire life, or do you want to live a little? You told me you had fun on the snowmobile and can't wait to be in his Mustang, hanging on for dear life and screaming your lungs out while going too fast around a mountain bend. So, at twenty-nine, it's more about deciding what you want for the rest of *your* life."

"Yeah, I think I get that."

I grab my purse, trench coat, and keys and drive to the arena. The fact that it's lit with purple lights makes it easy to find. There is a humongous TV monitor and an outdoor bar they opened for tonight's game, and people are sitting on lawn chairs listening to the live music. This is much nicer than any tailgate party in the parking lot.

I like the vibe, and I'm excited because soon I'll see Wyatt. Everything will be okay once I see him on the ice.

In the meantime, I pick up my ticket at the will-call window and make my way to the Clubhouse level, where my ticket is scanned. I see a room that opens onto a balcony, a full bar in the back, and a long food table.

I make my way into the room, surprised to see other women my age and older. There are about a dozen women, but it's not just wives. It's mothers, too.

I take off my coat and lay it over the back of a chair. When I turned around, a woman approached, takes me in her arms, and said her name was Jodi, and she was so happy to meet me.

Jodi! That's Wyatt's mom! She hugs me, and I melt in her arms. I'm so touched, I well up with tears, happy tears. I don't know if he planned this- well, of course he did. He had to know his mother was coming.

"It's so nice to meet you." I give her the biggest, warmest hug I've ever given anyone in my life.

"Wyatt's told me so much about you. I couldn't wait to meet you. We're so happy he found you. He's so happy." We make our way to the balcony and find two seats together.

We talk like two long-lost friends finding each other after twenty years. While Jodi tells me things about Wyatt I did not know, I see Charlie staring a hole through me out of the corner of my eye with her minions. From the puss on her face, you'd think someone in her posse just farted.

Meanwhile, a younger woman comes up to us and introduces herself as Cynthia. She's dating one of Wyatt's teammates, and I ask her to join us.

"Look, it's hard being the newest member of the WAGS," she says, sitting beside me.

WAGS?

She sees the confusion on my face. "Wives and girlfriends, you've never heard of it?

"I thought it was just a TV show."

"No, it's real, but you might want to watch the show to immerse yourself. But I got you." She gives me a hug. "I'm a girlfriend, too, but I'm not like the others. Stick with me. We're going to have a good time tonight."

And indeed, we do. The Maulers won, pushing us closer to the fourth position in the league. Mom and I meet Wyatt after the game, and we go to dinner with some of his teammates and their mothers.

It took my entire life to realize that I don't need to be alone. Before now, I would push people away, but now I'd rather be a part of something, especially if it involves Wyatt.

27

WYATT

I'm in the locker room, and we're all in a great mood after our win. A few other guys flew their mothers in for the game, and we decided to go to a pub across from the arena to decompress. It's impossible to sleep right after a win. I have no problem sleeping before a game. In fact, I took a nap earlier, so I'd be well rested, just like my teammates.

Our schedules are weird, but we get to do what we love. We might sit in the penalty box for no good reason, and then again, we might deserve it. We all spend our fair share of time drawing a penalty or inflicting pain on someone else when it's needed.

It's hockey, and I'm so glad Emily enjoys it.

I meet up with Mom and Emily, and they look as chummy as all get out. It makes me smile knowing the two women I love are hitting it off. I can tell my mom is giving us her seal of approval. The only reason Dad isn't here is because it's girl's night, but he will come soon enough, I'm sure.

The night air is filled with the cheers of boisterous fans as the last few are heading to the same pub. We reserved a private room for that very reason. I don't want to risk anymore tabloid mug shots.

Although a few pictures the reporter took came out so nice, I had one printed on a canvas, and it will arrive any day.

I've decided we need a more dog-friendly home for Mika and that a house might be my next investment, as long as Emily is fine with it.

I can't believe the online tabloids ran an article calling her a gold digger last week. Next week, they'll be clamoring for more pictures of us. How soon they forget, but such is life.

We had a great night, and Mom stayed with us for the weekend. Emily made us all cappuccinos with chocolate in them, and we took turns cooking breakfast for Mom. Emily did her signature French toast one morning, and I did blueberry pancakes the next morning. Mom was impressed I knew how to flip a pancake. I told her she's not lived with me for a while and that I outgrew hot pockets a long time ago.

I CAN'T BELIEVE that the April fundraiser is right around the corner. The past three months have flown by. I'm young, maybe a bit crazy, all hockey players are, but I don't see why so many guys wait years to get engaged or spend years engaged, getting married only to have kids.

Where is the romance, I ask myself?

Emily has had challenges with some of the women, but she found a friend, Cynthia, who is dating another player on the team. They sit with each other at the home games and have a girl's night when the team is out of town.

Emily is making it work, but it helps to have your family and friends behind you. It made my life easier when my parents never gave up on my dream. It doesn't hurt that I had an uncle who played college hockey, so my dad wasn't surprised when I took to skating so well the first time on the ice. I was three years old.

Mom was terrified I'd get hurt, but in their wisdom as parents, they knew it would be a hit or miss. There is no in-between, and they were right.

Emily thinks we're meeting up with friends for a boat ride on Camden Bay. This morning, I got up early to pack a small backpack of water along with a backup battery for our phones. We have a bit of a ride by car, but it's not too bad.

We're going to be away all day. A neighbor who will take Mika out for us.

Emily wakes and I have her mocha frappe ready and bring it to her in bed.

"Morning, thank you so much." She stretches her arms over her head before taking what I call her desert-for-breakfast drink.

She sucks some down, and I point out she has some chocolate in the corner of her delectable mouth which she slowly and suggestively licks.

"Oh, you can't do that, babe." I adjust the boner in my tight jeans that show off my junk and my cute ass. Don't judge, she loves it.

"We have a big day ahead but don't worry, Jim is coming over later to take Mika out for us."

"What is it with you? Too much caffeine? You're buzzed. I thought we were meeting the gang today for a boat ride."

"We are, but I want to get there early."

"Okay." She stretches her long legs over the side of the bed. "Ugg, my legs are so damn white, I can't stand it!"

"We'll get a place that has a sun deck, maybe by a lake. We don't have sandy beaches but there are tons of lakes here."

She stands, and heads to the shower. "That sounds nice. God knows I don't miss the Miami traffic."

She showers, puts her hair up all cute, like she does, and dons a grey shirt and jeans. She crawls around the closet floor and pulls out the boat shoes I made her get last week.

"This lake house you're promising me needs to have a huge closet," she continues.

I sneak a peek at my watch. "I'll just take Mika out a minute, then we'll head out."

"Okay." She puts on her no-show socks and her L.L. Bean boat shoes. Now she looks like a proper New England boater.

I return, putting Mika in her crate and Emily has our Maulers hats and sunscreen.

"I don't know why I bother with sunscreen. I don't think I can get a tan this far north," she teases as we walk out the door.

I HAD the Mustang delivered this morning and she squeals when she sees it.

"Are you kidding me?"

"Nope, but we seriously need to get you your own cool car."

"This is so awesome," she slides in and looks as sexy as fuck in my car, another thing we need to initiate.

The drive to the coastline is fun, and we take some tight turns. Pulling into a huge parking lot, we see a large boat at the dock. It looks like a fishing boat, and it used to be one, but now it's used for other things.

I open Emily's door, and she gets out, looking around, "Wait, where is everyone?"

"Well, I had to get you here for the surprise."

She thinks about that for a minute.

It's whale season!" she exclaims as she throws her arms around my neck and practically knocks me over. "This is awesome!"

Within an hour, we are out in the ocean and walking around the deck, enjoying the scenery. I'm not religious but I still say a prayer that we have a perfect day. I open a bottle of water that we share, and out of the corner of my eye, I see a whale breach the surface.

"There it is," I exclaim, and everyone on the boat runs to my side. I worry that we're going to capsize. The captain makes an announcement that we have a pod of migrating whales off the port side. Little late buddy, and why doesn't he say left side for those of us who don't know the difference between port and starboard?

We're close enough to hear their blow holes and when Emily spots the babies in the pod, she is beside herself with excitement.

It's pandemonium as everyone tries to take pictures and selfies in a limited space in a limited amount of time. Next time, I'm chartering a private boat and bringing my parents.

I remember I need to make a picture eBook for her. I'm probably better at it anyway. Growing up with all this new technology, I have more experience with the latest apps.

The whale trip is a hit and after this, I take her to a well-known lobster place on the water. Mainers are pretty laid back, and more interested in boating than clothing, so there is no dress code to worry about.

"So, what do I owe to this occasion? I mean, I realize you can easily afford this but, did I miss the day-we-met anniversary?" She asks, her interest piqued.

I don't want to be too obvious by ordering a bottle of champagne, so I ask the waiter to bring a Prosecco. "Nope, I don't think so. Can't I spoil you just a little?"

"Sure, but do you think I'm stupid?" she scoffs.

"The furthest thing from it."

The waiter pours our bubbly, and we order crab stuffed mushrooms for an appetizer and lobster for dinner.

"This is amazing," she says, in between bites of the mushrooms.

"Just wait til the lobsters get here," I inform her.

"This Maine, it's growing on me." She gives me her sexy bedroom eye look and sips her alcohol suggestively.

I'm so getting fucked tonight.

"Well, there is an anniversary you missed."

"What?" There's panic in her voice, and I feel bad.

"Well, you don't know about it," I start.

"Okay…"

"You're confused."

"Oh, hell yes," but she smiles, and I have a feeling she knows it's coming.

I pull the ring box out of my pocket.

"Emily," I get down on one knee and open the box, "Will you marry me?"

"Wholly shit!" She giggles, covering her mouth with her hand, "Yes! Yes, I will, Wyatt Hildebrand!"

I slip a three-carat diamond on her finger. I can't have her with the smallest ring with that crowd. This is another area where size is important.

"It's gorgeous." She ogles it on her finger, clearly happy with my selection. "I love it. How did you know I'd like it?"

Mom, Natalie, and Cynthia."

"Oh, now I know why they were asking me all those odd questions." We laugh about it together.

Now I can order a bottle of Dom to celebrate.

Follow up with Wyatt and Emily's Bonus Scene

or https://geni.us/RookieinLoveBonusScene

Meet more team members in Jagged Ice Book 2 Please leave a review with just a click of a star! The next page has free chapters of Italian King. It's dark mafia but very contemporary!

TEAM ROSTER

TEAM ROSTER 2021-22 (subject to change)

C-Kal Kohlman #5, "A" Alternate captain as per Jagged Ice.

C- Jacques Bellare #65

C-Austin Martin, pronounces Maratn #38 is his lucky number

C-Eric Thomas #96

C- Finn Callahan #71

RW-Sean Ian #57

RW-Victor Karlsson "C" for Captain #90,

RW-Alexander Holloway #23

RW-Raymond Frick #73

LW- Wyatt Hildebrand #19 nicknames Hildy, Broomhilda

LW- Albert Bennett #86

LW-Sidney Roy #98

LW-Chandler Ross #49

D-Justin Puljujar #55

D-Colton Cermak #62

D- Simone Korhomen #77

D- Blake Gibson #45

D-Trevor Espisito #41 born April 1

D-Devin Coyle #68

G-Luc McDavid #23 f (or Patrick Roy)

G-Jason McKinney, backup #30 which is Martin Brodeur's number.

RESERVES

F-Greg Coture. #87 for Crosby, his idol as a kid

F-Douglas Wright #8 for Ovchekin

F-Michal Mitchell "#94 M&M" "Candy"

D- Georgiev Laurent #82 "Laundry" and at night "Dirty Laundry"

D-Roy Crug # 71 "Croog" is how it's pronounced

NHL TEAMS FOR THE SERIES

The NHL Team list for the Maine Maulers Series *subject to changes

Atlantic Division

Fort Myers Gators (Jackson: Against the Boards)

Buffalo Blazers

Boston Sharks

Detroit Brawlers

Jacksonville Titans

Ottawa Kings

Toronto Twisters

Wyoming Wolfs

Metropolitan Division

Washington Devils

NJ Bandits

Philly Flames

Carolina Cobras

Montreal Mounties

Nashville Legends

NY Renegades

Central Division

Calgary Oilers

Chicago Blizzards

Colorado Bears (Jackson: Against the Boards)

Dallas Bucks

Pittsburg Rockets

Quebec Pioneers

St. Louis Archers

Vegas Bobcats

Pacific

LA Thunder (Coach: Isak Sin Bin Series)

Edmonton Enforcers

Minnesota Mayhem

Phoenix Diamondbacks (Liam: The Enforcer)

San Diego Defenders

Seattle Whalers

Vancouver Cougars

Vegas Predators

ALSO BY ZOE BETH GELLER

The Sin Bin Hockey Series

Tyler: Hooked (Free prequel to the series)

The Sin Bin Hockey Series

Jackson: Against the Boards

Alan: Between the Pipes

Erik: Fire and Ice

Blayze: Slap Shot

Paavo: The Defender

Spencer:Penalty Box

Isak: Coach

Kaden: Game Time

Liam: The Enforcer

Jake: Roughing

Box Sets

The Sin Bin Hockey Series Box Sets

The Sin Bin Hockey Series Box Set Books 1-4

The Sin Bin Hockey Series Box Set Books 5-7

The Sin Bin Hockey Series Box Set Books 8-10

Maine Maulers Hockey Series

Maine Maulers Hockey Series

Rookie in Love

Jagged Ice

Hotter than Puck

Benched by the Nanny

Puck in the Oven

Pucking the Team Captain

Zoe Beth Geller's Hockey Pond Fan Group

Maine Megaladons (Football)

Faking it with the Football Star

The Player's Obsession

Volkov Brava

Volkov Brava (Standalone)

King's Promise

Brutal Promise

Sinful Promise

Dirty: The Micheli Dark Mafia Series

Dirty: A Dark Mafia Romance Series (Micheli Mafia)

Italian King A Dark Mafia Romance (Micheli Mafia) Book 1

Dirty Vengeance A Dark Mafia Romance (Micheli Mafia) Book 2

Dirty Bargain A Dark Mafia Romance (Micheli Mafia) Book 3

Dirty Born: A Dark Mafia Romance (Micheli Mafia) Book 4

Dirty Deals: A Dark Mafia Romance (Micheli Mafia) Book 5

.

Dirty Series Dark Mafia Fan Group

FREE SAMPLE OF ITALIAN KING

Download your free copy here!
https://geni.us/FreeItalianKingsample

ACKNOWLEDGMENTS

I have to give a shot out to my fans. Yes, fans! You humble me. It's taken me a long time for me to come to terms with the fact that I have fans who happily wait for my next release.

You stuck with me during my first series when I was starting and learning and I appreciate you so much. I strive to make each book better written and push myself to the limit in order to grow and hopefully bring you more engaging stories to read.

So thank you from the bottom of my heart for your messages, your emails from the NL when I mention I wasn't feeling well and for being you! It's all those acts of kindness that keep me in there on days I'm over worked and stressed out.

ABOUT THE AUTHOR

Zoe Beth Geller is an emerging hockey romance author. Her first series, The Sin Bin is a collection of 10 standalone novels but there is a bit of continuity across books and the changing of players and the beloved Coach. From the first bar where Jackson and Olivia kick off the series to the players coming into and leaving the team, readers will notice life and the town in Colorado are forever changing.

Her spin-off series, Maine Mauler Hockey Series is a pro team series based, obviously, in Maine! These are interconnecting romances that can be read as a standalone but this series has more team interaction between players and a series arc as well and would be best read in order.

Other works by Zoe include her dark mafia novel, Italian King, which is book 1 in Dirty: Dark Mafia Romance Series followed by Dirty Vengeance. These books can be read in order or standalone however, they are interconnecting with an overall series arc over 5 books.

Stay connected with Zoe through her newsletter with updates on evolving news and releases at Newsletter sign-up

For your free book to the Sin Bin Series download Tyler: Hooked

Fan Groups
Zoe Beth Geller's Hockey Pong
The Dirty Series: Dark Mafia Romances

www.ingramcontent.com/pod-product-compliance
Lightning Source LLC
Chambersburg PA
CBHW060411310726
48976CB00003B/1010